"Damn vultures."

Carrie slipped her feet into the green plastic thongs and marched to the apartment door. A mumble of voices drifted up and she stood quietly on the landing. The front door was ajar, lighting the figures below.

"Mrs. Rayborn, Lisa Wong here. May we have a few minutes of your time? Since we spoke on Sunday night, your daughter has been released to your custody. Can you tell us how you feel about the D.A.'s inference that there might be an arrest soon in the Hawkins case?" The woman thrust the black mesh top of the field microphone toward the stairs.

"I think things must be pretty slow for both you and the district attorney if the best you can do is innuendos," said Carrie. She turned and walked with intentional dignity up the stairs.

"And so you have another piece in this puzzle that surrounds Clifford Hawkins's murder." The sound trailed off behind her as Carrie pulled the door shut, slid the lock into place, and pounded her fist on the cluttered table.

# A CASE OF LOYALTIES

## Marilyn Wallace

BALLANTINE BOOKS  •  NEW YORK

Library of Congress Catalog Card Number: 85-25141

ISBN 0-345-33965-7

This edition published by arrangement with St. Martin's Press, Inc.

Manufactured in the United States of America

First Ballantine Books Edition: January 1987

For Bruce—
my love, my loyalty,
and this book.

The author is grateful for the support and encouragement of Betty Hodson, Polly Masters, Terry Shames, and the Saturday Group: Joan Cupples, Lucy Diggs, Kermit Sheets, Elizabeth Stewart, Katy Supinski, and (especially) Caroline Fairless.

# PART

# 1

# SUNDAY

# 1

She hadn't planned to steal a car but there it was, a big white beautiful Buick with the lights out and the engine running. The whole night had been filled with surprise packages. First the graduation party, wrapped in bright winking colors but on the inside just another beer-and-dope bash with everyone trying to out-outrageous everyone else. She had a beer, shared a joint, and left, ticking with excitement. As she walked through the streets she heard the stars sing, notes disappearing into the blackness.

The car was waiting just for her. She drove for a while, turning onto new streets at the last minute as if to trick herself. When she slowed for a stop sign she spotted Angela and enticed her with a tale of easy travel, a ride to continue the celebration. They would cruise a little, maybe open it up back near the warehouses, and then leave the car somewhere. Angela hesitated but Tricia said it was time to have some fun.

They turned the radio up loud and almost didn't hear the crash, except that the tinkle of glass and the crunch of the fender biting into the base of the lamppost couldn't be ignored. Tricia giggled and squinted, slapped her hand on the soft fluff of the steering wheel cover.

"Oh shit, should've worn my glasses. Everything's all wavy and blurry."

"Just back up and let's get out of here, okay?" Angela fingered the lapel of her blue blazer and slid back, pressing her spine into the seat.

"Hey, Angie, I've got a good idea. Let's park right here for a minute," Tricia said, trying not to laugh. "I believe I need another hit." She fished in the breast pocket of her jacket and pulled out a crumpled joint. "Another hit, get it?" she asked. "Did you see my lighter?"

"Come on, Tricia, let's go," Angela pleaded, but it was too late.

The reflection in the rearview mirror made Tricia dizzy. Her head was trying to follow the spinning red light, but her stomach felt as if it belonged to a different body, going in another direction. She looked at the steering wheel to steady herself. "Just be cool," she warned. "We'll get out of this. No problem. We just have to stick together."

And then the Man was standing beside her window, rapping against the glass that had been rolled up to keep out the Oakland night. He was wearing a blue uniform and he had a gun in his hand.

# 2

It was a little before nine and Carrie Rayborn had no appetite for dinner alone. She waited in her studio for the foam at the top of her second glass of beer to settle down.

"Stupid," she muttered to herself. "Morrisey's got to be terminally stupid to think I can't see through all his posturing. Expects us to be grateful and not ask for raises if he invites us to a goddamn catered lawn party."

A butler with receding hairline ladles champagne into crystal cups. Red and white awning billows above bosomy ladies with blue finger waves and filmy pink dresses, flutters over mountains of curly watercress and sweating cheese.

She tapped her right foot, the worn deerskin toe touching the same spot on the floor. When Jim Morrisey had hired her, Carrie assumed that working four days a week as a bookkeeper at his insurance agency would leave her time and energy to paint on the other three days. The money wasn't enough to support them, really, but she was certain a painting would sell soon.

She stepped closer to the canvas. The suggestion of a figure emerged from a cloud of mauve that drifted into a harder-edged dancing line near the lower right; it needed a transition to connect it to the central image. She drank the beer without stopping for a breath and stood back.

"Thinks he can buy off an entire office of underpaid workers with a few drinks and some soggy sandwiches," she said aloud, although there was no one to hear her.

She pushed back a fine strand of light brown hair and reached up to adjust the flaps of the rigged ceiling lamps. The stooped old landlord had been proud of the front room, called it The Parlor, but she claimed it for her studio. It was the only room in the flat with three high windows, wonderful unobstructed north light. Four shelves, a large and a small easel, and her paintings filled the space now. The smaller paintings, a series done in celebration of her arrival in California four years ago, were abstract, as her earlier work had been. But her palette had changed, reflecting less and less the haze of East Coast light. The recent work was bigger, colors washed by cloudless skies. Now, even in the dark, she brought out hoarded memories of light, basking in the savored warmth.

"Why does she do this to me? She promised she'd be back early to finish her homework. She was only going to Angela's to talk." Carrie wandered into the living room, an eight-by-eight-foot alcove between the stuido and the kitchen, and opened a copy of *Images and Issues*. "All I want is to make paintings, sell a few every now and then, and spend the rest of the time laughing and talking with my kid about how goddamn wonderful the world is."

We wear white dresses. A straw hat shades my eyes from the sun. Round marble table, glasses of iced tea, each with one perfect green mint leaf. My hands fly, Tricia's eyes widen, as I finish my story.

Carrie lit a cigarette and tossed the match into an ashtray without checking to see if the shot was good or even if the match was out. She stepped into the kitchen and balanced her glass on the breakfast plates, which rested on two cups, considered the pile in the sink, and decided in favor of the canvas waiting in the studio. As she passed through the alcove again, the telephone rang. Marty. She had forgotten.

"Hello," she said, an edge of impatience in her voice.

"Hi! Well, are you in a good space to look at the tape?" His voice was cheery even when he was staring, intent on his work, through the lens of a video camera, or stretching after a ten-mile bicycle ride. Carrie knew that a mere pause wouldn't be enough of an answer; his persistent ebullience might interpret anything as affirmative.

"Listen, Marty, can we do it another night? Tomorrow's Monday and I didn't get anything done all weekend. I just started to paint and I don't feel like company, okay?" The long phone cord moved with her as she carried the receiver into the studio and stared at the canvas.

"Sure, kiddo," he said. "Stardom can wait." His laugh was easy. Carrie envied that in him.

"Hey, you were the one who wanted to make a tape of Artist-at-Work. It wasn't my idea."

"I'll be glad to take all the credit," he said. "So when can we check it out?"

"How about Tuesday night? Maybe by then I won't feel like such a leftover." She smiled.

Me on a plate in the refrigerator, a little gray around the edges, wrapped in Saran with a piece of soft carrot resting against my cheek.

"Sure, kiddo, sounds great. You know," he added, "I love the way the tape captures the creative process, all those sensual images, the brushes. And your body language. Terrific. It really works."

Spare me, she thought, as she stepped back into the living room in anticipation of the end of the call.

"And I'll even bring a marvelous little Chardonnay I discovered. Great balance of oak and spice."

"A party. I'll have two glasses washed by eight o'clock. See you then."

She hung up, knelt down, crawled under the table, and paused. Surely Tricia would breeze through the door any second now. She unclipped the plug from the wall receptacle. The movable, disconnectable telephone was one of the few real improvements that modern technology had made in the quality of her life.

"Goddamn interruptions. Who can paint? Music, that's what I need." Carrie mumbled, turning toward the rear bedrooms. The albums had been in perfect alphabetical order a week ago, although it had always been difficult to decide whether Taj Mahal belonged with the *T*s or the *M*s. She pulled out the first Janis Joplin she came to. Under the *L*s. She lifted the playing arm, blew a clot of dust from the needle, and set it down. Then she stretched out on the bed, eyes closed, and sang along.

Pink feather boa swirls and long gold earrings swing as I stamp my feet. I look over the microphone. The crowd seethes, jumps, ripples with the music.

A loud noise startled her and she sat up, annoyed. Firecrackers, she thought. Goddamn kids with firecrackers or a car backfiring . . . or a gunshot.

The racket of shouts and cries from the street made her uneasy. The loudest voice sounded like Mrs. Donnigan. Carrie got up, straightened the seam of her jeans, and strained to make sense of the commotion outside. By the time she reached the kitchen, she was considering the possibilities.

'She's all right, safe. She's at Angela's. Talking about graduation, boys. Kid stuff. She's fine. Just a little late."

She ran the last five steps to the studio window.

Carrie scanned the pools of light cast by open doors and street lamps, looking for Tricia and finding everyone else. Mrs. Donnigan's orange hair stuck out as if she had fallen

asleep on the sofa watching a rerun of "M★A★S★H."
Clutching her faithful green cardigan with one hand, she
pointed to the corner of Renwick Street with the other,
jabbering and waving. Mr. Wilson was trying to get her to
slow down by holding his huge hands out to stop the stream
of words. Four boys wearing *Star Wars* shirts circled across
the street in front of 1228 Fairfax Avenue on their bicycles,
pointing at the figure that lay face up on the broad white
porch, the edges of a pool of blood darkening to the same
color as the black man's skin. Two young men shouldering
barely portable tape players lounged against a red Corvette.
Sounds began to take shape.

". . . maybe a Caddie or a Buick, with a white
dog . . ."

". . . got the license plate number . . ."

". . . called the cops and an ambulance . . ."

Ordinarily Carrie would have turned away, as she did
from those television interviews with bereaved relatives of
undeserving victims. But this was her street. Someone had
been shot and Tricia wasn't home. She was probably out
there, standing in a doorway. Carrie grabbed her keys and a
cigarette and ran down the stairs.

Her eyes moved quickly up Fairfax from the corner
grocery past her door to the Stop sign at the intersection of
Renwick. No Tricia. A girl with a short brown bob, right
hair, wrong clothes. What was she wearing when the left the
house? Red high-necked sweater. No, the white sweater and
that oversized man's jacket, collar turned up and sleeves
pushed to the elbows. Gray jacket, pants, too, but a darker
tone.

Carrie checked the second-story windows, passing over
the light filtering from her own bedroom into the studio, and
saw a collection of backlit faces, but no Tricia. Her
breathing slowed and voices again separated from the buzz
of the crowd into words.

". . . and they should have thrown him out after . . ."

". . . a dog in front, a poodle with patches of black around both eyes, and . . ."

". . . stayed out of his way. Don't need no trouble here. Get enough of that when I make deliveries to . . ."

". . . hit his heart, I bet. Can't never get blood out, whole porch has to be painted. My aunt told me . . ."

Against her will, Carrie stared at the house, its shades drawn like eyes shutting out the sight of the bloody body. Blue paint was peeling around the window trim and a section of rain gutter was missing. The driveway cement was cracked, but the grass had been cut recently and the hedge beside the walk was clipped, neat and square. No different than all the other houses on the block. She turned away and headed for the corner.

Six minutes later, an ambulance and three police cars drove up. In the confusion, Jack Tate, half crocked and hoping for a party, was knocked into the fire hydrant in front of 1226, and lay sprawled on the sidewalk as blue uniforms and white uniforms rushed around, clearing spaces and setting up barriers, shouting at the crowd to stay away from the porch. The mob dribbled away. No one liked being questioned by the police, and it was getting chilly.

Only a few people remained, and Carrie looked again for anyone who might know where Tricia was.

"Royal," she called to a slight young man with wire-rimmed glasses, a heavy book held against his chest.

"Good evening, Mrs. Rayborn," he said as Carrie approached. His eyes followed the trickle of medics and policemen, and he started to walk away.

"Wait a minute, Royal. Have you seen Tricia?"

The young man looked at the porch. "No, I haven't." He stared at a blond man in a dark blue suit who grabbed two startled onlookers and stuffed them into the back of a patrol car. Frank Nelson and Belinda somebody, Carrie thought. Witnesses, probably.

"What are you doing around here tonight?" Carrie

asked, looking over a group of whispering girls near the grocery store. "I hope nothing's wrong with your grandmother."

"Oh, she's fine," Royal said. "I'm developing my endurance. I walk the mile and a quarter from my house to Grandmother's every other day. Mental strength and physical strength—they work together." Carrie followed Royal's distracted gaze to the patrol car. The blond man opened the door, and Frank and Belinda, pale and silent, walked away.

"That's really admirable, Royal. I wish Tricia had some of your discipline."

The orderlies pushed a gurney down the walk to the open door of the ambulance. Carrie couldn't imagine that the shape under the thin white sheet had been alive, just twenty minutes ago.

"Terrible, isn't it," she said.

There was no answer. Royal stared at the door of the ambulance as it slammed shut, his mouth open slightly. Carrie shook her head and returned to her own side of the street.

She hoped to remain invisible long enough to make it back inside. Maybe Tricia was trying to call; maybe her San Francisco gallery was phoning right now to say that they had sold *Aquaterrine* for $1,500. Better get upstairs and plug the phone back in. She squeezed between Jack Eldridge and Mrs. Llobante, who still had some customer's skinny eggplant clutched in her small brown hand, and submerged herself in the clump of women gathered in front of her house.

"Did you see the car, Miz Rayborn?" the silver-haired African violet lady asked.

"Sorry, Mrs. Washington. I was in the back room listening to music."

"What about Tricia? She see it?"

Carrie shook her head and opened the door. Her arms felt like two long kazoos, humming with the breath of no song in particular, buzzing through to her shoulders and on into her neck. All the vibrating collected just above her eyes, then traveled back and forth across her head. Her tears were hot.

Someone was dead, shot in the night. Some mother's child had been murdered. Hers was still alive.

# PART

# 2

# MONDAY

# 3

Oakland Police Headquarters was fluorescent-lit, a cold and pulsing light that made everyone look one-dimensional and green. Behind a window in the reception area, a policeman clutched a telephone between his right ear and his shoulder. Carrie tapped on the glass, wishing that she had called Marty or someone, anyone, to come with her. The thought disturbed her; she could handle this. She shifted gears.

"I'm Carrie Rayborn. I got a call about my daughter Tricia. She . . ." Carrie searched for the words. "I'm here to see Sergeant Cruz."

"Just a minute, miss." The man scratched at a tuft of gray hair poking out from his left ear and formed letters on his pad. "Perpetrator's description?" He wrote again.

They must have talked her into it, Carrie thought, or maybe it was a dare. Never had been one to turn down a challenge. Where do they put little girls who are accused of stealing cars, she wondered.

Tricia huddles on the floor in the corner of a large cell, her knees under her chin. Three women in short black skirts and high heels, blouses tight, nipples erect, point at her and smile, lick their lips at her inexperience.

The officer replaced the receiver and began to copy words from one sheet of paper to another. Carrie put a hand on the sill of the partition.

"Now will you please call Sergeant Cruz?"

The man shrugged, punched out four numbers, and mumbled into the mouthpiece. Standing straight, Carrie waited, ignoring the round old lady snoring on the bench. The elevator chunked to a stop and crisp footsteps approached.

A kindly Walter Matthau policeman, big mustache, rumpled suit, walks through the door with an arm around Tricia and apologizes for the mistake.

The glass doors swung open and an angular man, tall and thin-lipped, wearing a well-cut dark blue suit, walked toward her. He didn't look like a Cruz.

"Mrs. Rayborn?"

"Yes. Sergeant Cruz?"

"He's my partner. I'm Sergeant Goldstein."

She examined his blue eyes. A Goldstein?

Goldstein takes off his perfect clothes, reveals a transparent body, a lucite casing that houses pulleys and cogs but no blood or organs or glands.

"I was expecting Sergeant Cruz. He called and said that my daughter is being held here. Car theft and possession of marijuana."

"Yes, that's right." His voice was without age or accent.

"I want to see her. Where is she?" The old lady on the bench grunted and pulled her arms in close to her body. "She's probably very scared."

"There may be another charge, Mrs. Rayborn."

"What do you mean? What other charge?"

Goldstein cleared his throat and smoothed the knot of his tie. Manicured, she thought. I've got a manicured policeman.

"We still have some checking to do," he said.

What else could it be? Running a red light? Driving

without her license? Big deal. "Look, when can I see Tricia?"

"They're almost finished. She's upstairs in Juvenile, fingerprints, pictures, that kind of thing. Why don't we wait in my office?"

Carrie fell into step beside him as they walked down the corridor past several unmarked doors. Rounding a corner, they approached a door with very clear black letters that said HOMICIDE. She looked around for another door but there was none. They were at the end of the hall. He must have made a mistake, walked right past his own office, she thought. Dumb cop.

His hand was on the doorknob; he belonged there. This wasn't happening. She wasn't really standing in the middle of an office with no windows, into which eight large desks were crowded. Goldstein led her to a tiny room with a table and two straight-backed chairs.

"What other charge, Sergeant Goldstein?" She felt the wooden chair against the back of her knees and sank into it.

"Can I get you some water?" Goldstein pushed his chair away from the table. Carrie shook her head and he laced his fingers together, resting folded hands on the tabletop. "Someone was shot from a car at nine-fifteen tonight, across the street from your house." Carrie nodded. "About twenty minutes later two girls were found in a car that had the same license plate as the one witnesses saw on Fairfax. Your daughter was driving that car."

His eyes were still focused on a spot about two inches to the left of her nose. Carrie felt pierced; she leaned into the chair for support, rubbing the smooth arms. Her face was hot, and a trembling began in her shoulders and shuddered down her arms in brief attacks.

"Did she . . . do you . . . ?" She put two fingers against her lips, pressing them closed.

"We haven't found the weapon yet, and Tricia says she never drove up Fairfax. Right now, we can't charge her."

"What's going to happen to her?"

Goldstein's voice became even more matter-of-fact. "Tricia will be held in Juvenile Hall until tomorrow afternoon, when there will be a hearing to determine whether she'll be tried as a juvenile or an adult."

Carrie tried to swallow. "I'd like that drink of water now. How can she be tried as an adult? She's only seventeen."

Goldstein stepped into the larger room, pulled a paper cup from the dispenser and pressed the blue button on the water spigot. He held the cup out to Carrie.

"Seventeen is a legal no-man's-land," he said. "It's up to the referee. He considers the nature of the crime, her past history, that sort of thing."

A man in a black and white striped shirt and white knickers, cap jaunty on his balding head, raises his arms, fist toward his face. Personal foul. Fifteen yards.

"Referee?"

"Ambiguous title," Goldstein agreed. "He's really an appointed judge."

"I'm going to call my lawyer." Carrie brightened at the thought of action.

The telephone rang in the other room. Goldstein answered it, said only "Right" and hung up.

"You can see Tricia now," he said.

Carrie followed Goldstein to the fourth floor and through a door marked JUVENILE. A dark-haired man sat at one of the desks, bent over a pile of papers. He looked up when the door opened, his eyes brown, warm, and sympathetic.

"Mrs. Rayborn, this is Sergeant Cruz." The man rose and rolled down his shirt sleeves, buttoning them as he walked toward Carrie.

"Where's Tricia?" Carrie searched the room. At least there were four windows here, even if they were covered by metal grids. Everything was neat—little black plastic cubes on each desk for paper clips, plastic cups for pencils and pens, the typewriters covered with plastic hoods.

"Sorry I couldn't meet you downstairs, Mrs. Rayborn."

"Please, just let me see her." Carrie heard the ice in her voice. Good, she thought. Better ice than quivering panic. Goldstein pointed to the door at the other end of the room. She walked slowly and concentrated on making her face relax. Angela and Tricia sat behind a table, chairs close, holding hands and saying nothing. Angela's face was pale, Tricia's flushed.

"Trish."

Tricia looked up, then back down at the table. Her mouth made tiny tight lines, lips moving together and then not quite apart.

"Tricia, are you all right? Please look at me."

The girl's eyes swam with confusion. Carrie went to her, wanting only to gather and protect her child, to sing her sweet songs and feed her warm milk. She put her hand on Tricia's shoulder and the girl grew rigid. Carrie pulled back; even now, Tricia wouldn't relinquish her world-defying guardedness.

"What happened, baby? I thought you were just going over to Angela's."

Tricia stood up and leaned against the wall, feet crossed at the ankles. Her fingers rubbed the frayed hem of her jacket. It was comically big; her body was lost in it.

"Did they talk you into it, Trish?"

The girl's head snapped up and she almost smiled. "No one ever talked me into anything in my life." Her green eyes gave nothing away as they fixed on the tops of her shoes. "You want to know what happened? I didn't think you'd let me go to the party because I had that report to finish, so I told you I was going to Angela's." Carrie looked over at the table. Angela swayed a little, as if she were trying to correct for the motion of a gently rolling ship.

"And then?" Carrie asked.

Angela turned away and rested her head in the circle of her folded arms.

"We just partied a little, drank some beer, smoked some dope, and took the car. So what. Then these cops come and tell me that they think I killed someone." Tricia pulled a flip of hair down onto her forehead. "Oh shit, I just want to go home and go to sleep." Turning the middle button of the jacket between her thumb and forefinger, she hunched her shoulders inward and bent her head.

"Look, Tricia, I'll be back in the morning, as early as I can, but they told me you're going to have to stay in Juvenile Hall tonight."

"Yeah, they told me, too. Used their fucking police words, thought they would confuse me. Remand and incarcerate and all that crap. Can I get some clean clothes? Would you bring my tan cords and the blue shirt?" A flicker crossed Tricia's face as she resumed twisting the button and tapping her foot. Carrie couldn't tell if it was fear or pain, but Tricia's wall had shown a chink, a crack of vulnerability. Carrie was comforted.

"Sure, Trish. Anything else?"

"No, but if Twink calls tell him that I'll see him in a few days and that I've taken care of the problem."

Carrie's chest rose and fell rapidly and a sticking dryness returned to her throat.

"You took care of the problem?" Carrie said. What else don't I know about your life? she thought. A typewriter clacked in the other office, and Carrie, unaware of Cruz standing in the doorway, watched Angela reach out and take Tricia's hand.

"I'd like to talk to you for a minute, Mrs. Rayborn." Cruz was gentle as he steered Carrie toward the hall, touching her elbow, leaning forward to hold the door open. His voice was soothing, and she knew that he intended his words to be helpful.

"Okay," she said, "I can see that she's reacting to all

this. I'm upset, too. You know, you people are making a lot of assumptions. Stealing that car doesn't make my daughter a murderer." She filled her lungs with smoke, exhaled, and watched the blue curls twist toward the globe hanging from a narrow tube. Cruz put his hands in his pockets and leaned against the wall.

"Angela said they were at a party, drinking beer and wine and smoking marijuana." He spoke slowly and the words began to make sense. "She said that Tricia left the party alone, at about ten to nine, best she could remember. Told us Tricia was bored and wanted to find Twink."

"That's her boyfriend, Richard Cavellini."

He is touching Tricia's arm, his black hair sparkling sleek and long, eyes glinting as he gestures, teeth shining as he laughs. Alive electric energy surrounds him in blue and white crackles.

Carrie looked for an ashtray, found none, and crushed the cigarette under her foot. She picked it up and stuffed it back in her pack, watching Cruz's eyes, which were nearly black as he returned her gaze, talking to her without words.

"Thank you for going slow with me," Carrie said softly. Cruz nodded and continued.

"Angela said she left shortly after nine. She was on her way home when Tricia pulled up in the Buick and asked her to go for a ride. They ended up smashing into the light pole."

Carrie's eyes followed a trail of scuff marks down the speckled asphalt tiles. I still don't get it, she thought.

"So what did Tricia say?"

"Oh, her statement fits with Angela's," Cruz said. "She left the party and walked around looking for Twink. Says she took the car at about twenty after nine. She told us that the motor was running and that it was parked on Foothill Boulevard." Cruz inched closer to the Juvenile Division door.

"So I don't see the problem. How could she have killed anyone from that car at nine-fifteen if she didn't take it until nine-twenty?"

"She was pretty stoned when she was picked up, Mrs. Rayborn," Cruz said. "We think they were mistaken about the time. The owner called in to report the car missing at eight fifty-four. Says he went into the Stop 'N' Buy on High Street. Ran in for some bread. He left the engine running and when he came out the car was gone."

She finally understood.

"I know this is hard." He pushed away from the wall and opened the door, signaling to his partner. Carrie waited as they filed out, first Goldstein, then Tricia, then Angela.

"It's going to be okay, Tricia. Try not to worry."

Tricia hesitated and swallowed hard. Carrie held her for a moment, startled by how small her daughter felt. We can just run from here, Carrie thought, down the stairs out onto the street. We are protected, it will be all right. Tricia pulled gently away and stepped into line behind Goldstein.

Carrie watched the small group disappear, one by one, around a corner, then stepped woodenly to the elevator. The UP light flashed, the door slid open, and she got in. Hitting MAIN, she reached up to draw her scarf close to her throat; it wasn't there.

A roll of blue and gray wool sitting on the lacquered orange arm of the bench, watching over the old lady bundled in her black coat.

Carrie pushed the button for the second floor. A quick stop at the reception area, get the scarf, go home.

There it was, where she'd left it. She picked up the scarf and began rummaging through the aging leather bag, once delicate and fawn-colored. Her head hurt and she couldn't remember why she was digging around in her purse. The hall seemed to dim and shrink.

"Hey, miss, what's the matter? You better sit down." The

man scuttled from behind the glass partition in time to steady Carrie with two papery hands. She kept her eyes on the blue ropes and knots of veins on his hands as he led her to the bench.

"Thanks," she whispered, "I'm all right."

"Yeah, and I'm Ronald Reagan." He reminded her of Uncle Benny, the dry cleaner.

"I'll be okay in a minute. Thank you. Really."

He turned away, shaking his head as he nudged the door open. Carrie realized that she had been looking for her car keys and stuck her hand into the purse again, squaring her body and aligning her neck with the imagined plumb line she visualized to restore herself. As she felt around at the bottom of her bag, footsteps clicked on the floor and then stopped. A young woman wearing a green silk dress, her chin-length hair turned under at the ends, stood looking at her. Carrie tried to remember if she had ever worn anything that was real silk. No, she didn't think so. A lot of cotton in her past but no silk. The woman marched directly to the bench. Carrie knew her, she was certain, but from where? She ran through a catalog of places and experiences and came up empty.

"Hello. My name is Lisa Wong. You're Patricia Rayborn's mother, aren't you?"

Map behind them, curve of tan countertop in front of them. They are delivering the news. The man is adjusting his pale blue collar. The woman is smoothing her dark hair, touching her red silk blouse, wide mouth moving with the words.

"I don't have anything to say to you." Carrie's fingers found the key ring and she stood up.

"How old is your daughter, Mrs. Rayborn? Do you know what reasons she might have had to shoot Clifford Hawkins?" Lisa Wong produced a small bound notebook and a mechanical pencil. "Did you know the boy yourself?"

"You're invading my privacy, Miss Wong. I already told you that I don't want to talk to you."

"Has Patricia ever been in trouble before?"

Carrie was at the double doors. She put one hand on the cold metal frame and turned. "There's no Pa. It's just Tricia." Carrie repeated the line she and her daughter had used for years, ever since Isaac had left. "And you're opening yourself to a libel suit if you report that Tricia killed Clifford Hawkins or anyone else. You better go get a fucking law degree and get yourself appointed judge if you want to have a say in it."

The sight of her old blue Valiant on the deserted street was reassuring. Even a battle with the temperamental ignition seemed like a friendly activity, everyday and appropriate. She drove home slowly, stopping for all the lights.

# 4

Goldstein examined the figure. The crested helmet indicated a dragoon, an officer. The plume was bent back at the tip, and the waistcoat, in regimental colors of dark green and saffron, reached almost to the top of the over-the-knee boots. He would finish painting the other soldiers, four carabineers, tomorrow. Then he had to mark the terrain—hills, streams, woods—and the structures, mostly farm buildings, on the folding game board. And buy the brandy. Preparations for the next semi-annual simulation of the Napoleonic Wars were almost complete. Of course, Thompson and Kimball, buddies from his two years at Stanford, insisted on drinking Courvoisier VSOP as they moved painted lead soldiers across painted wooden country-side. They worked hard at suspending disbelief.

"They even killed each other according to rules," he said, stroking the metal plume feather.

Cruz tilted his chair and propped his feet on the half-open bottom desk drawer. "Hey, man, if there were some rules out there," he said, pointing his head in the direction of Seventh Street, "that would make our job easier, no?" He riffled the small pad in his hand. "Well, at least it's Monday and Morella and Price get the new cases. Should be a slow week. All we gotta do is find out how the Rayborn girl got the gun and where it is now."

"Isn't that a little premature?" Goldstein asked, lining the figurines in a staggered row on the green desk blotter. "There are still pieces missing. The weapon, for one thing, and then there's the matter of a motive for another."

"We'll get it," Cruz said, turning to look at the clock above the doorway. "Guaranteed. Not more than twenty-four hours. By seven-fifty-three tomorrow morning, we'll be done. Hawkins was one righteously nasty dude. There's a story between him and Rayborn and we'll find it. Today."

Goldstein pushed the dragoon to the other side of the manila folder and stood the remaining figures in an opposing rank. "Okay, I know about Hawkins. Hardworking gas station attendant transformed into the terror of the neighborhood. Maybe there was something between him and the girl. And maybe," he said slowly, "it's one of the other stories. You're starting with your conclusion, and, *a posteriori,* looking for the facts. We have to be more objective."

"I *am* being objective," Cruz said, voice loud. "It's a fact that she was in that car. It's another fact, man, that she got no witnesses to say that she was walking around the streets, eight blocks away." His thumbs began tapping, as if he were transmitting an urgent message. Goldstein met his stare.

"Take it easy, Carlos. You know, you sound angry, even a little scared. Maybe you're worried that your sons might blow it, like you think Tricia Rayborn did."

Cruz curled his thumbs under his fingers, holding tight and nearly shaking. "First I get your philosophy bullshit and now I get your psychology bullshit. Let's stick to the job, okay?"

"Hey, you guys see this?" Morella boomed, juggling coffee container, two bagels with cream cheese, and *The San Francisco Chronicle.* "Captain's gonna be A-number-one royally pissed. Glad it's not my case." He dropped the paper on Cruz's desk and waddled across the room to his own chair, pulled it out with his right foot, and plopped down. Goldstein pulled his chair around and read the article.

Page one, center column. He went straight to the second paragraph, skipping the usual lead information: victim's name and age, where and when he was killed. The reporter mentioned an Unidentified Juvenile, and went on to build a confusing hypothesis involving black, Latino, and Asian gangs. He ended with a thinly veiled call for a new clean-up-the-streets campaign. Not only would the captain be pissed, he'd probably be all over them.

"Yeah, well, some asshole reporter doesn't bother me," Cruz said. "We got a good handle on this one, man. Just a few more things to check out. Day or two, it's all over." He smiled and Goldstein's forehead wrinkled.

Morella's grin lifted his large ears, and his eyes sunk deeper into the folds of fat that had once been cheeks. "So who is it?" he asked, mouth full of half-chewed bagel, cream cheese, and coffee. "Your unidentified juvenile?"

"That's how I see it, Tony. The kid was in the car that the shots were fired from. Gang action, my ass."

Morella looked at Goldstein for confirmation.

"Well," Goldstein began, his frown deepening, "there are some other—" He was interrupted by Price, Erikson, and Webster, bounding in with hands full of containers and newspapers.

"Hey, Cruz, did you know that you're a, quote, 'veteran Hispanic detective with a softspoken manner and gentle eyes,' unquote? That's gonna boost your image." Erikson's teeth gleamed as his lips stretched in a thin smile. Price folded his gray windbreaker across the back of his chair and stood watching the action.

"So who did it, Cruz, the kid in the article?" Webster asked.

"Yeah, that's how it looks. She was in the car, she was

stoned, and she got no alibi." Cruz maintained an even voice as he turned to Goldstein. "Right?"

Goldstein didn't look up. "It's a possibility," he said, picking up a folder and shuffling papers purposefully.

"Hey, Goldstein, how's your daddy gonna like this line? Quote, 'Detective Jay Goldstein, noted for his dapper dress and the son of a well-known Marin County attorney, said that it was too early to reach any conclusions,' unquote. You gotta say you know, even if you don't, professor." Erikson continued smirking. Goldstein thought that if the man took a sip of his coffee now, it would pour out the sides of his mouth.

Morella scraped the chair backward, heaved his bulk to a standing position, and trundled around to the front of his desk. "All right, don't you guys have any work to do?" He dumped the empty cup and crumpled wax paper into the metal trash can. The door opened again, and Delvecchio and Murdock entered, pink-faced.

"Well, if it isn't old Gentle Eyes." Murdock paused, batting his lashes in Cruz's direction. Delvecchio reached up, pulled his shirt sleeve from beneath his jacket cuff, and patted an empty handkerchief pocket, performing in front of Goldstein's desk.

"Hey, this is getting old fast," Cruz said, lobbing a pink eraser halfway across the room, watching as it bounced into Erikson's IN basket.

Delvecchio leaned both elbows on his own cluttered desk and rested his chin in his hands. "So how you gonna feel, putting another one away? You two have been real hot stuff this year. Seven out of seven so far. The juvenile, huh? How old?"

No one answered.

"Hey, Goldstein, that's not a hard question. How old is the kid?"

"Seventeen," Goldstein replied softly, "but we don't have a case yet."

"It won't be too bad for her," Cruz said. He shook his head, a wedge of brown hair falling across his forehead into his browner eyes. "Being a girl, that'll probably help her. Auto theft. Manslaughter. A good lawyer will put her in a skirt, show off her school record, and the referee will go easy."

"Only she's not being charged with murder yet," Goldstein said. The room was still. The other six detectives looked over to Cruz, who sat biting an already well-chewed pencil, turning it slowly. "Let's go, Carlos. We have a a lot to do." Goldstein stuffed papers into his desk drawer, Cruz returned a folder to his wire basket, and everyone watched them.

"Hey," Morella began, "me and Webster, two years ago we almost didn't talk to each other over that Donut Delight case, you know the one where someone busted into that doughnut shop and waited for the girl who opened up in the mornings and shot her face off. God, what a mess, she had this bloody hamburger for a face. Webster said it was the boyfriend, she had just broke it off with him and"—Cruz put his jacket on—"I was sure it was a hit-and-run robbery, some guy surprised at how early she was there, but"— Goldstein picked up the carabineers and put them in the top drawer—"it turned out that it was really the other waitress, a nut job, boy, a real nut job, but see, it didn't matter whether Web and I agreed or not because we were both—" The telephone rang. Morella stopped in midsentence.

"Homicide. Detective Cruz." Cruz looked over at Goldstein. "Just a minute." He held his hand over the mouthpiece. "It's the captain's office." Goldstein watched as Cruz shook his head, said "Yessir" four times, and hung up.

"Did he say anything I can't already guess?" Goldstein asked. Cruz grinned, shook his head, and walked quickly to the door. He sprinted down the hall to the stairs, Goldstein following close behind.

\* \* \*

Goldstein swung his six-year-old BMW onto the Nimitz Freeway, grateful that the department car to which they were entitled was down for a brake job. It smelled.

"Hey, man," Cruz said, rolling up the window as papers started blowing on the backseat, "the way I see it, there must've been some number that went down between Hawkins and Rayborn. Drugs, or maybe he pushed too hard on one of her friends."

"And she decided to dispense some personal justice?" Goldstein asked, picturing a tableau of old men and olive trees.

"Yeah, maybe. Or maybe the marijuana shorted her fuses . . . Hawkins made a real good target."

Traffic was light and Goldstein stayed in the slow lane, heading south past the drydocks and warehouses. "Look, we're not adversaries. We have to keep our priorities straight or the whole case will be in jeopardy. We have the same goal. We have to find out who killed Clifford Hawkins." Cruz stared out the window. "You said that you heard some other stories last night, when you were talking to people on the street. Let's go over them."

"It ain't much, let me warn you." Cruz pulled his notepad from his pocket. "First, I got the name of an Annie something, maybe Matson or Marsten. I can't read it." He squinted at the letters, held the pad closer to his face, then moved it to arm's length. In the field, he wrote in a personal shorthand that sometimes defied even his translation. "Never mind. I'll get it later." Cruz drew his shoulders up. "See how you like this. Annie is seven. Just a baby, really. This old janitor comes out into an alley to dump the trash, finds Hawkins pulling down her pants . . ." His words trailed off. "Animal."

He turned to the next page as Goldstein pulled around a slow-moving truck with a badly painted salmon on the side panel. "The only other thing is a Mrs. Franklin. Got knocked down and broke her leg. The guy grabbed her Social Security check and split. She thought it was Hawkins." Cruz flipped the red cover over the pages and put it back in his pocket. "That's it."

"See," Goldstein said. "Those two stories are worth following up on. And I want to find out more about the boarding house where Hawkins lived. There's something strange going on there."

Cruz grinned and raised his eyebrows.

"Not like that," Goldstein said, gathering memories, sifting impressions. "Last night I spoke to John Kim Soong and Miguel Santos. Soong is an electrician's apprentice and Santos works for one of the trucking companies down near Jack London Square." He slowed to allow a silver Porsche to move into his lane. "They told me the names of the other boarders." He paused, shifting down and letting the Porsche put another car length between them. "Listen to this. Burwande Mumbabe, Nguyen Tho Doc, and the manager, Ali Khamir."

"Sounds like our own little United Nations right there on Fairfax." Cruz looked down at the folded newspaper on the seat beside him. "Gang action, no way. Those guys probably just need a cheap place to sleep. The only other reason a bunch of guys like that would live together is if they were in the army, man."

"You see," said Goldstein. "The possibilities are expanding. Who knows what any of those people in that rooming house had against our friend Hawkins? I'm not ready to lock the girl up yet."

"And I believe that while we're out here chasing around, she's gonna go down to the station and confess. The car, remember."

"Truth, Cruz. Capital T. Stay objective." Goldstein signaled and swung the car onto the ramp at the High Street exit. They sat in silence, passing rows of pastel stucco houses. He almost overshot the turn onto Fairfax, and Cruz muttered a protest as the tires squealed softly. Goldstein braked and recovered, found a parking place in front of the grocery store.

"Okay, so I'm gonna check out Annie and that Mrs. Franklin and you're gonna go over to the rooming house," Cruz said, his hand on the dashboard. "Let's meet at, say, one o'clock, back here."

Goldstein looked at his watch and checked the side mirror before opening the door. "Make it twelve-thirty. I have to take care of something downtown this afternoon. How about ribs for lunch?"

"No way, man," Cruz answered, passing his hand over the second button of his jacket. "Something easier, like maybe Chinese. Hey, what about that Szechuan place over on . . ."

Goldstein grimaced and waved.

# 5

Only a pale brown stain remained where Clifford Hawkins's blood had soaked into the white porch boards. Goldstein reached out to knock on the front door just as it opened. A wide-mouthed John Kim Soong stood in front of him.

"Oh, sorry, Sergeant," the boy said, "I didn't expect anyone to be right here." He waited, half in and half out of the doorway.

"No work today?" Goldstein smiled.

"Well, I had some things to do," Soong said as he patted the ribbed waistband of his crewneck sweater, "so I'm going in late."

"Is Mr. Khamir in?" Goldstein stood squarely in front of the door. The boy frowned, and then his face became expressionless.

"I can check for you."

"Why don't you do that," Goldstein said, moving quickly past Soong into the entryway, "and I'll wait here."

The boy started to say something but, with his mouth still open, walked up the stairs, turning at the landing to look back at Goldstein. Two large curved arches flanked the hall. Goldstein peered through the one on his right into a square and unremarkable room. Two curtainless windows faced the street, dull beige shades pulled halfway down. The sofa, a green and gray striped affair, was pushed up against a wall, and the three wing chairs had identical grease spots nestled among the faded blue and pink cabbage roses on the headrests. A mahogany coffee table with curved legs stood in front of the sofa while a taller matching table separated two of the chairs. Both tables were bare. No books, no magazines, no litter.

Jay Goldstein moved back into the hall and stood at the foot of the stairway, listening. Soft voices drifted down from one of the rear rooms and footsteps paced rhythmically. He stepped closer to the other arch and looked into the dining room. A large table and eight chairs sat in the middle of an imitation Oriental rug. More beige shades, pulled halfway down. Goldstein entered the room.

On the wall opposite the windows were two maps, secured at their ends by transparent pushpins stuck into the plaster wall. The one on the left was a detailed rendering of the city of Oakland, the other a larger, regional map. Several thick yellow lines highlighted routes from Oakland, Berkeley, San Francisco, San Rafael, and San Mateo, each ending at a bridge or a landmark. One line moved from a residential section of north Berkeley to the Lawrence Museum of Science in the hills above the university campus. Another followed Highway 101 to a spot just west of the Marin County entrance to the Golden Gate Bridge. His heart pounded with the memories of the concrete bunkers guarding the entrance to the harbor. The San Francisco line ran from the Richmond district to Coit Tower atop Telegraph Hill. Proper strategic choices—as the real estate people say: location, location, location. His brain buzzed, fixing the markings, fitting the yellow lines into a pattern.

A door slammed upstairs and Goldstein took a final sweeping glance at the dining room before moving quietly back into the hall. He stood facing the staircase, his back to the dining room arch, and followed the progress of Soong's

Nikes and a pair of polished penny loafers as they came down the stairs.

"Detective Goldstein, this is Mr. Khamir. Excuse me. I have to get something from the kitchen and then I have to go to work." The boy walked off down the shadowed hall.

"Pleased to meet you, Detective Goldstein." The man who spoke was not more than five feet five, but his body appeared hard and muscular. His eyelids seemed weighted, half closed under thick black lashes. He was dressed in what appeared to be the uniform of the house: corduroy pants, light shirt, and dark sweater. It was a preppie United Nations, by the look of it.

"I have a few questions, Mr. Khamir, and I want to take another look around."

The small man smiled and inclined his head. "Certainly. How unfortunate, that young man being shot right here." His voice was deep and he spoke softly, licking the bottom of his luxuriant mustache at the end of each sentence.

"Tell me, how long did Hawkins live here?" Goldstein took two steps backward, closer to the dining room.

"About a year. He was already here when I came to manage the house last July." The man was so cordial. But his smile extended only as far as his mouth. Khamir shifted his position gradually until he was facing the dining room, then moved back and leaned against the living room arch. A struggle for territory, thought Goldstein. To keep me away from the dining room?

"I understand he had some problems lately, in the neighborhood." Goldstein was aware that his skin felt damp under his clothes. Khamir took another half step back and Goldstein joined the dance by moving in the opposite direction, closer to the dining room.

"Until three months ago, everything was fine," Khamir said. "Then there were some, ah, difficulties. He was, shall I say, a troubled young man." His tongue swiped twice at his mustache at the end of that speech.

"Do you know what brought about the change?" Goldstein asked.

Khamir smiled. "I make it my business to stay out of the personal lives of the men."

"Is this your house, Mr. Khamir?"

The man's eyes grew large. "What do you mean?"

"Do you own this house?" Goldstein asked, wondering whether the uncertainty was cultural, semantic, or a play for time.

"No, this house is owned by a corporation. I'm just the manager. Now, if you like, I can show you upstairs. I must leave soon to keep an appointment." He tilted his head and the corners of his mouth turned up.

"Fine," Goldstein said, "this won't take too long. By the way, what's the name of the corporation?"

"What corporation?" Khamir asked.

"The corporation that pays you to run this house, the owners."

"Oh, they are named Oneida West," Khamir said, turning his back to Goldstein and starting up the stairs.

The stairway was without dust, even in the corners. When they reached the second-floor landing, Goldstein paused. Nothing of note here. A small telephone table, complete with old-fashioned black rotary dial phone, a pencil, and a pink message pad. Six doors, all closed. A worn red-and-blue braided rug. No pictures and no maps.

"Here it is," Khamir said, holding the door open. "Although I suppose you remember from last night. I will wait downstairs." He bowed and retreated, a thin gleam of moisture glistening on his forehead.

The walls were white, the room spare. Anyone, from a maiden aunt to a mad poet, might have lived here. A mirror hung above a brown boxy dresser; the bed was covered with a brown cotton spread; a clock and a lamp with a dimestore shade stood on the nightstand. Jay Goldstein opened every dresser drawer for the second time in thirteen hours. Shirts folded and stacked, sweaters folded and stacked, even socks divided into whites and colors in the top compartment. He slid the night table drawer open. No unpaid bills, no letters from friends, no comic books. In the closet, five pairs of corduroy pants, a gray jacket, and a black raincoat hung neatly, and two white towels were folded over a bar on the door with military precision. He thought about the other bedrooms, barren and interchangeable, except for shoe sizes. Go slow, he warned himself, and take notes. He wrote rapidly, listing impressions and questions, then went downstairs.

Khamir was standing in the living room, hands clasped behind his back, when Goldstein came in. "Is there anything else, Detective?"

"I just want to have a quick look around down here," Goldstein said, "and then you can go to your meeting, Mr. Khamir. Keep yourself available for the next few days."

"Certainly," Khamir said.

Goldstein walked quickly through the spotless kitchen, then into the living room, and murmured a low "Excuse me" as he stepped around Khamir into the dining room. On the wall opposite the shaded windows hung a cheap framed reproduction of *The Peaceable Kingdom*. The maps were gone.

Carlos Cruz peered through the flowered curtain in the door window, following the progress of a bent figure as it approached. Bump, step, shuffle, pause—repeated until a thin voice said, "Yes?" and the curtain was drawn aside.

"I'd like to talk to you, Mrs. Franklin. I'm Sergeant Cruz, Oakland Police."

"Hold on there, young man," the piping voice warned. "You don't look like no policeman to me."

Cruz stepped back so that the dark eyes could see more

than his jacket; he pressed his shield to the window. "Here's my badge, Mrs. Franklin. This won't take very long."

A safety lock was undone, the brass knob turned slowly, and the door opened. A tiny white-haired woman in a white-collared blue dress, thick white stockings covering her spindly legs, leaned on a carved cane.

"Body can't be too careful these days, least not an old old body like me." Cruz nodded in agreement. Her hair was short, the tight curls still dense in contrast to the slackness of her wrinkled black skin. "Sometimes people just go away before I can get to the door." Her smile drove a network of lines into a bunch around her eyes. "Why, Lordy, where's my manners? Come sit down in the front room." She turned carefully and proceeded to a cheerful room lined with shelves, miniature cups and saucers sprouting from every surface, and hobbled past a low table to a wooden chair with stenciled yellow flowers climbing up the backrest.

Cruz explained the purpose of his visit. The pleasant, self-contained peace left the old lady's face, replaced by a scrunching scowl.

"That boy. I know it's not charitable of me, but he wasn't no good."

"What do you mean, Mrs. Franklin?" Cruz waited while she completed a slow sorrowful shake of her head.

"It was like he was one of my own grandkids. Well, not really, but he would stop to help me with my packages. We sat some afternoons and had lemonade here on the porch. Then, when all the trouble started, he was like another person."

"What trouble do you mean, ma'am?" Cruz asked.

"Oh, my accident, and the poor little Marsten girl, and that Jimmy Jackson. Clifford said Jimmy was looking at him funny. Can you imagine? Beating up that sweet boy so bad he couldn't go to work for a week, 'cause he thought Jimmy looked at him funny?" She went on shaking her head as she spoke, reminding herself of her disapproval and disappointment. Cruz copied the names into his pad; there might be time today for two more interviews.

"What about your accident, Mrs. Franklin?"

The old lady shifted painfully in the chair. "Now I never said it was Clifford. All I could see with these old eyes was a shirt, a blue sweatshirt, like the one Cliffie had." She smiled graciously, apparently enjoying the chance to chat. "I went to get the mail, out there on the porch, from the new mailbox my daughter got me for Christmas. It's the holidays I look forward to, Christmas and Easter and Halloween, all the kids so excited."

The back door opened and then closed softly. According to his information, Mrs. Franklin was a widow who lived alone. He reached his arm across his chest, shifting so that he felt the reassuring weight of his gun beneath his jacket. When he heard a glass clink and the refrigerator door open, he relaxed. Probably a neighbor who looked in on the old lady.

"Someone just came in the back door, Mrs. Franklin. Do you want me to see who it is?"

"Lordy, that must be Royal already," she said, as a boy of about nineteen appeared in the doorway carrying two glasses of milk with a plate of cookies balanced on top. The family resemblance was obvious: the same narrow frame, the same smallish mouth, and the same wide-set eyes behind wire-rimmed glasses. Cruz had a vision of what this studious-looking young man would look like when he was much older.

"Morning, Grandma." He bent down to kiss her wrinkled cheek.

"Sergeant Cruz, this is my grandson Royal. He's only nineteen and getting straight As over at Mills College."

"Oh, come on, Grandma. Sergeant Cruz doesn't care about me. No bragging," he said. Mrs. Franklin's eyes shone with pride.

"I know what you mean, Mrs. Franklin. I feel the same way about my sons. I'm their soccer coach, and when we practice down at the Redwood Heights Rec Center, it really makes me feel good to see how well they do, what good sports they are."

"He's always telling me about the interesting things he's reading. Like that Russian fellow—what's his name?"

"I'm sure Sergeant Cruz didn't come here to listen to me talk about Dostoevsky, Grandma." He looked at Cruz with a shy smile.

"Can't help it, honey. It makes me feel so proud." She looked at Cruz knowingly.

"I was just asking your grandmother about Clifford Hawkins and her accident," Cruz said.

"She's still not completely recovered, are you, Grandma?" Royal ran his fingers along the shaft of the cane and gripped the carved head.

"How did it happen?" Cruz asked, still looking at Royal. The boy was obviously upset about the accident.

"Well, I'll tell you," Mrs. Franklin said. "It was just before Easter and Mrs. Evans, she's the nurse next door, she was gonna take me to the five-and-dime to get baskets and such for the kids. I like to get a brooch or ribbons for Jessica, and the boys, well, I wasn't sure about Thomas, but Royal, I was going to get him a special bookmark. Leather and all. First in the family to go to college, you know." She beamed at the boy. "I was waiting for my Social Security check. Mostly, my mail is bills. Scandalous how they charge more and more."

"You know why she waits for her Social Security check every month?" Royal said, leaning forward to the edge of his chair and resting the cane against the low table in front of the sofa. "She puts half of it into a trust account to pay for my education, don't you, Grandma?"

"Was your check in the mail?" Cruz asked. Mrs. Franklin nodded slowly.

"See, this fellow just ran up onto the porch and grabbed all the mail. He gave me a hard push and I fell down. Can't imagine how it happened, but I heard a funny pop and, Lordy, there I was pointed one way and my leg pointing the other. Old bones, I s'pose." Her eyes watered but she couldn't seem to squeeze enough moisture out of her dry old body to actually cry. "No Easter presents for the kids, that was what was so bad." Her eyes crinkled. "But they are so good. Jessica said not to worry, that they would find a way to get money for the lights and food, and Thomas told me never mind, having me for a grandma was the only present he needed, and Royal just stood looking all wise and said that God works things out right for the good folks and that I was the best."

Cruz wondered when the good folks were going to learn that they had to be smart, too.

Royal got up, took his grandmother's hand, and looked directly into her eyes until the sad memory left and a smile crept into the corners of her mouth again.

"I think she better lie down for a while," he said.

"I understand. You take it easy, Mrs. Franklin."

She was still smiling when Royal led her to the sofa and Cruz let himself out.

Goldstein waited in the car, scanning the *Chronicle* story for the third time. He could see the pained expression that would come over his father's face when the wiry old man read his name. True justice, Goldstein thought, remembering his father's mouth, pinched and white with fury when Jay announced at the end of his second year at Stanford that he planned to teach philosophy, recalling the voice screaming that Aaron Goldstein would pay tuition for a future lawyer, a future state senator perhaps, but certainly not for a future teacher. He relished his father's shocked disbelief when he took the tests for the Oakland Police Department.

Fortunately, Jay loved the work. The only real drawback,

so far, was the money. Metaphysically speaking, he had concluded that events were the manifestations of beliefs, so he lived as he wished to, materially speaking. Of course this took some sleight of hand, careful selection, and a lot of credit card maneuvering, but it was all working out.

The passenger door opened, and Cruz and his Coca-Cola settled into the seat.

"Your turn," Goldstein said as he eased the car into the quiet street.

"Sure. First the old lady. If my grandmother was putting me through college, I'd be watching out for her health, too. Her grandson stopped by. Good kid. Be nice if Carlos Jr. and Julio had some of his . . . his . . . I don't know."

"Fine. Now, what about Hawkins? Anything?" Goldstein asked.

"Well, the old lady thought it was Hawkins who knocked her down and stole her check, but she's not sure." He drained the last of the soda from the can. "The Marsten family wasn't home, but I got one more story to check." He crushed the can in his hands and turned to look at Goldstein. "Jimmy Jackson, lives around the corner. Mrs. Franklin said that Hawkins beat him real bad, said that . . . 'Jackson looked at him funny' were her words." Cruz squeezed the can, compressing it with loud popping noises.

"Charming gentleman, our friend Hawkins," Goldstein said. "Fine example of the civilizing effects of society, wouldn't you say?"

"So maybe Rayborn was just taking care of cosmic business," Cruz offered.

"Not necessarily the girl taking care of business," Goldstein said. The signal flickered to green and he edged around a van waiting to make a right-hand turn.

"You still don't believe it, man?" Cruz turned the crushed can slowly. "You got a better bet?"

"Maybe. That boarding house gets more interesting. When I got there this morning there were two maps on the dining room wall, local maps. They had these strange yellow lines. Weird. By the time I left, someone had taken them down."

"I'm telling you," Cruz said, "it was Rayborn."

"Rayborn," Goldstein repeated, angry. "That sounds like some hard-assed con from Quentin."

Cruz looked out the window as Goldstein switched on the radio in time to catch the closing chords of something familiar, Mahler, he thought. They drove in silence, side by side, apart.

Out of habit, Goldstein gave a half salute as they passed Mills College. Before it became coed, he used to wonder what it would be like to teach there. All those bright young girls, cloistered away among the birches and maples in their mini-Massachusetts. Something nice and not too esoteric like, say, Jamesian pragmatism, and to be thoroughly conscientious, stay after class now and then with a student who needed extra help. He directed his thoughts back to 1228 Fairfax. A very characterless cipher of a house, populated by polyglot blue-collar workers and one dead ex-inhabitant who seemed to have gone off the deep end lately. Cruz interrupted his thoughts with a mumble.

"What did you say?" Goldstein asked.

"I was just wondering what was going to happen to her. I wish I was wrong, but I still think she did it. All we have to do is find out what he did to her and we'll have the answer.

# 6

Carrie sat on the gray plastic chair beneath a cheap paper print of orange and brown badlands baking under a cruel red sun. Notices were taped to the metal frame that separated the mesh-reinforced glass overlooking the hall. Seven people sat in identical gray plastic chairs, some bored, others appearing frightened, none looking as if they wanted to be there. No one spoke. One large woman, the hem of her plaid dress coming undone in the back, rocked in a chair, eyes staring into emptiness, an occasional sound making its way from her throat.

Carrie fidgeted with her cigarette pack, trying to recall the details of the early morning phone call. The Public Defender had answered her questions with curt replies, and most of the conversation was a hazy blur. Tricia's hearing was to be one of the first, and the lawyer advised that she was going for juvenile status. This would mean no jury trial. She had assured Carrie that the referee would be easier on Tricia than twelve people with unpredictable biases.

A banquet-sized table, oak chairs pushed away. Coffee containers ringed with lipstick, filled with cigarettes, soaked and black. Crumpled sheets of yellow lined paper heaped on the floor.

Cool air brushed her face, and Carrie looked up to see a man with an Alameda County Sheriff's Department patch on his blue shirt standing in the doorway.

"Did you say Rayborn?" she asked, half rising.

"Clayton. Family of Jane Clayton?" The man was young, not more than twenty-five. His polished hair shone under the lights and a gun hung heavily in its holster on his hip. Carrie sat down and swung her foot back and forth. What had Jane Clayton done? Would she be going home with her mother to live a normal life? No one responded to the call for Jane's family. Where were they? Carrie worried for the girl. Maybe Jane Clayton has committed some terrible, vicious crime. She lit another cigarette and the door opened again. "Agnes Jones. Family of Agnes Jones." No one stood up. The fat woman and her friend started an argument over whether it was better to use lard or butter in pie crusts. Carrie realized that she hadn't eaten since sometime Sunday afternoon. It was now 1:35 P.M., twenty-four hours later, Monday already, but there was no room for hunger in the knot that was her stomach.

She rose, stretched, stepped into the hall. A stocky man walked toward her, a tan trenchcoat slung over his arm.

"Mr. Martinez," Carrie said, pleased at the thought of company. "I'm so glad to see you." The man stared at her. "Listen," she offered, "the lawyer says we have a really good chance for this to work out for the girls."

"We?" the man said, his eyes narrowing. "There is no *we*, Mrs. Rayborn. My Angela didn't steal a car, she didn't have any marijuana in her jacket, and she was at a party when that boy was killed. No *we*. You just remember that." He held her gaze for a final moment and then walked into the waiting room, pacing with jumpy little movements back and forth behind the last row of chairs. Carrie looked at him through the glass, clenching her jaws hard. The muscles in her temple tightened into a massive headache.

The sheriff's officer reappeared, pushed open the door to

the waiting room, and said, "Is there anyone here for Tricia Rayborn?" Carrie waved and followed him through a heavy door into a small courtroom.

Tricia was seated at one end of the table, carefully examining her wristwatch. Her face was drawn and the dark circles under her eyes made her look rather less like a child. Once again, Carrie was swept by a need to leap the barrier and cradle her child endlessly, but she moved to a seat in the first spectator row, closest to Tricia.

"It's going to be okay, Tricia. Don't worry," Carrie whispered. Tricia looked up, her face still pinched. A tiny glint of recognition and relief sparked in her eyes.

The man opposite Tricia, hidden behind piles of thick folders, stood and said, "Are the parents of Tricia Rayborn here?" Carrie felt panic. Should she stand or raise her hand or say that only the mother was here? She rose without deciding to, like a child in a classroom, and said, "I'm Tricia's mother," and then sat down. She had a brief choking sensation, as if everything were happening under water and in slow motion. She strained for air, barely hearing the muffled clicks of the court stenographer's machine. Look, she thought, I'm wearing stockings and a skirt, and my hair is in a bun. My daughter is pale and she is wearing a bra for the third time in her life. These things count. Oh please, thought Carrie, let me not break any rules I don't even know about. Let my instincts and the quality of my soul protect my child.

The lawyer had her back to Carrie and was talking to Tricia. The girl said "yes" in a whisper. The referee, behind a desk that was set on a raised platform, looked at the man with the folders. He was saying that Tricia's grades and attendance record were good. The pressure on Carrie's chest was increasing, voices gurgling in her brain. A man in a pinstriped suit was speaking now. Carrie struggled for air. Tricia turned to her, seeking her eyes, and Carrie fought to come back from the watery trance. Tricia needed her here, now, breathing and thinking and being present.

"And possession of marijuana," the man said with clipped enunciation. "This office would like the court to be aware that these charges may soon include murder."

Carrie looked at the public defender, expecting her to stand and say, "Objection, Your Honor." But the man went on. "Given the gravity of the situation, we must recommend detention at a state youth facility."

The waters receded and Carrie rose, talking calmly. "The charges against my daughter include car theft and possession of marijuana. This is not a murder trial." She watched the referee lift his gavel and went on hurriedly. "You can't go changing the rules because a young person is involved." Carrie looked at Tricia, whose face was full of gratitude and fear. "I'm sorry, Your Honor, but I just wanted to say that my daughter is not being charged with murder." She sat down, breathless.

"I was just about to object, Your Honor," the public defender said. "The references made by the district attorney are inappropriate to this hearing. I ask that they be removed from the record and that you ignore them in your considerations."

The room was quiet and the referee sat expressionless. His chest fell with a sigh and he said, "I agree, Counselor." Carrie smiled, hoping to catch Tricia's gaze and share the victory.

"Is it true, Tricia, that you have had no contact with your father for more than six years?" the D.A. asked. Tricia folded her hands in her lap as Carrie prickled with apprehension. What was the man up to?

"Not exactly," Tricia answered.

"Please speak up. What do you mean, Tricia?" His steely hair didn't move as he bent over his notes.

"Well, he sent me a card for my sixteenth birthday." She

rubbed her thumb along the table edge, avoiding everyone's eyes.

Tricia's elegant fingers methodically tearing the card into pieces, tossing them out the front window. Flakes floating weightless like ashes, lifting on the wind and never touching the ground.

Carrie was startled by the sound of the door opening. She turned and met Goldstein's eyes. Shivering with dread, she searched for some explanation of his presence. No, she thought, go away.

"All right, thank you, Tricia. Your Honor, it is clear that the family situation is unstable. The girl's mother has been unable to hold a job for longer than six months at a time. I must recommend that Tricia Rayborn be detained until her trial."

Tricia jumped to her feet. "My mother is a painter. She works for money at these dumb jobs whenever she has to, so that she can paint the rest of the time. But we always have plenty to eat and the bills get paid. She has rules that I have to follow, and she also taught me to stick up for what I believe. You can't make her out to be incompetent just because she hasn't bought into your way of doing things."

Tricia and Carrie looked at each other. Even across the half wall, they felt the strength of their bond, and were changed.

The referee coughed. "I need fifteen minutes to review," he said, and walked out through a door to the left of his desk. A tall gray-haired woman in a pale blue dress entered the room and crooked a finger at Tricia, who moved obediently toward a door that opened onto a room with dark cinderblock walls and a wooden bench. The door closed behind them, and Carrie remembered Goldstein. And she wanted a cigarette.

The corridor was empty. Carrie lit a cigarette and peered

into the waiting room. The fat lady sat slumped in a chair, her thighs leaking over the sides, mouth slack and eyes closed. Carrie was about to stab out the cigarette in the sand-filled standing ashtray, when Goldstein came around the corner. Implacable. A quality on the police ratings? He'd score high on that one.

"Good afternoon, Mrs. Rayborn." His eyes were shaded, more gray than blue now.

"Why are you here?" Carrie asked, trying to keep the trembling from her voice.

"Oh, for another case. I stopped by to see how things were going for you and Tricia."

"I'm not sure how to read the signals," Carrie said. "We've never done this before." Time to go back in. She didn't want to be standing here, amiably chatting with the man who might later arrest her daughter for a murder she didn't commit. "I'd be very grateful if you and your partner would do your job and find out who really killed Clifford Hawkins." Without waiting for further conversation, she turned and pushed on the heavy door, making Goldstein vanish, if not from her thoughts, then at least from her sight.

It was over for now. They filled out the endless forms, gladly. They listened, happily, to the explanation that home supervision meant that Tricia must come home every day from school, and not go anywhere unless she was accompanied by Carrie, until her trial, which would be in four weeks. Then they were out on the street, with buses and trucks and cars rumbling by. They hugged each other, neither laughing nor crying, assuring each other that they were real. Carrie felt the liquid rush of relief again seep into her muscles.

"Let's go home, Tricia," she said.

"Hey, Momma, can we wait for Angela? She was real scared last night. A big fat girl came on to her while we were in the bathroom brushing our teeth, and she was so scared. She started shaking and crying." She looked up the steps toward the door, as though the wish would make her friend materialize.

"What happened?" Carrie asked, unable to envision Angela recovering enough to ward off an assault.

"I told the other girl to fuck off, and she came at me with a belt wrapped around her hand, but she was real fat, so I grabbed the belt away from her and told her to leave us alone." Tricia looked fierce, and Carrie remembered the set of her face when, a head shorter than the others, Tricia played general to their infantry, ordering attacks and commending her troops for bravery, out in the weeds.

"Listen," Carrie said as she put her arm around Tricia, "I met Angela's father in the hall, before your hearing. He was real upset, very angry that Angela was dragged into this, as he put it, because of you."

"Yeah, well maybe that's how he feels, but Angela is my best friend and I want to wait for her. Let's hang out for half an hour, and if she doesn't come by then, we'll go home and I'll call her later." The clarity in her eyes made the request, earnest and reasonable, impossible for Carrie to refuse.

They sat together on the steps, watching the cars and buses, the trucks and vans, the taxis and pickups, the Jaguars and Fords and Toyotas. Neither woman looked at the passersby, as though there was more comfort to be gained from the movement of the insentient machinery, faithfully going, sputtering if necessary, but going on. After eight minutes, Angela and Mr. Martinez appeared and Tricia got up.

"Angie!" she said, breathless and awake again, smiling at the good fortune that she and her friend would once more share daylight and freedom. She ran up the steps and threw her arms around the other girl.

"Stay away from my house and my daughter," Mr.

Martinez said, roughly removing Tricia's arm from Angela's shoulder. Tricia cringed while Angela stared at the cement. Carrie felt a surge of fear, but there was nothing to be done.

"Tell her, Angela." The man's face hardened, his mouth barely open. You tell her now, so she understands."

Angela opened her mouth, but only a small choked sound escaped.

"Tss. Now!" Mr. Martinez let go of Tricia's arm and was holding Angela's shoulder in a pincer grip.

"I can't see you anymore," Angela said, in a voice that was too loud and had no inflection. "I . . . I can't even talk to you." She stood shaking quietly, her eyes filling as Tricia backed away. "So don't call my house or try to talk to me at school."

Tricia clasped her fingers together. "It's okay, Angie. I know he's making you say all this. I'll always be your friend." She reached up to touch Angela's face but before her hand made contact, Mr. Martinez yanked his daughter's arm and they went flying down the steps. Angela turned, her face shining with the need for forgiveness, and then they were out of sight.

There is going to be so much to explain, thought Carrie, including why some things can't be explained.

"Okay, let's go home. We can pick up some pizza." She wanted Tricia to start talking, to begin the cleansing so that it might be over. More likely, there would be a long period of quiet first.

"All right, Momma, but I don't want pizza. Let's just go home." They walked the half block to the car, and twice Carrie moved closer to make sure that their shoulders touched.

"Do you think that she'll listen to him when we're in school? That she won't talk to me?"

"I don't know, Trish, but if she does do what he says, then don't hate her for it. He's worried, and he's doing what he thinks is right, and she's scared, too. He's her father. I mean, don't take it personally." God, what a stupid thing to say, Carrie thought. Of course it's personal.

"Of course it's personal, Momma," Tricia said without challenge.

Carrie nodded. "You're right. As soon as I said it, I realized that I was wrong."

# PART

# 3

# TUESDAY

# 7

At 6:30 in the morning, compact brown sparrows and oversized jays, competing for the choicest berries, trilled and argued in transit from clothesline to treetop. Oakland day workers, counting on another ten minutes of sleep, grumbled and turned and finally tossed their bodies out of bed. Carrie went on dreaming of a pastel paradise teeming with round amethyst fruit and oval amber melons. Tricia sat on a beach, carving a point in a bamboo pole as one of the vines sprang up, wriggled to standing position, and draped a tan trenchcoat on its back.

She shivered and forced her eyes open. Almost 7:30. She groaned and pulled the covers up, lulled by the even, resigned sounds of Bob Marley on Tricia's radio. Five more minutes, she thought, and then I'll get up. She began to drift off again, when the downstairs bell blared. Angela, coming for Tricia to walk to school. No, not Angela, she reminded herself—the trenchcoat, Mr. Martinez. She heard Tricia amble to the front of the house and then back to the kitchen. The bell rang again.

"Whasat?" Carrie called from her bedroom.

"TV," answered Tricia through a mouthful of food. Carrie tried to focus on her daughter's figure, small and dark in the doorway. "There are some reporters and cameras and stuff downstairs. They rang the bell a couple of times and now they're knocking on the downstairs door."

Carrie propped herself against the pillow. "How long you been up?" She worked to get her mouth unstuck.

"About two hours. Couldn't sleep. The birds." Tricia chewed carefully. "Hey, can I stay home from school today?"

Carrie gruntcd as she swung her feet onto the floor and pulled the flannel nightgown down from her waist. She padded to the bathroom. A knock on the downstairs door turned into an aggressive pounding and then stopped. Mouth full of toothpaste, she stepped out of the bathroom, ready to call Tricia. The girl stood in the hall, still chewing.

"Don't answer it, okay?" Tricia nodded. Carrie finished brushing and gargling and splashing. "They still out there?"

"I'll go look. Wait a minute." Tricia went to the front window, standing far enough back to avoid being seen. "The truck is still there." Carrie emerged from the bathroom, her hair twisted and clipped into a knot at the back of her head, her eyes not yet working properly. She zipped her jeans as she stepped into the hallway and pulled the red sweater down over her belt loops.

"Goddamn vultures." She slipped her feet into the green plastic thongs and marched to the apartment door. A mumble of voices drifted up and she stood quietly on the landing. The front door was ajar, lighting the figures below.

"Well, the mother is a painter, single lady, nice but kind of, you know, well, maybe not so stable."

"What do you mean, 'not so stable,' Mrs. Thurmond?"

The paralysis of shock came and left quickly, and Carrie bounded down the stairs. "Yes, what *do* you mean, Mrs. Thurmond?" she said. The camera panned smoothly to the fifth step, pointing its blank eye at her, then back to the reporter. Carrie was too far from the light source and she waited, in small triumph.

"Mrs. Rayborn, I didn't mean nothing bad, just like, you know."

"No, Mrs. Thurmond, I really don't know." Carrie squinted to get a better look at the reporter, who was partially hidden by the man with the camera.

"Mrs. Rayborn, Lisa Wong here. May we have a few minutes of your time? Since we spoke on Sunday night, your daughter has been released to your custody. Can you tell us how you feel about the D.A.'s inference that there might be an arrest soon in the Hawkins case?" The woman thrust the black mesh top of the field mike toward the stairs. Her fingernails were long and red, and a dainty ring matched the string of pearls around her neck.

"I think things must be pretty slow for both you and the district attorney if the best you can do is innuendos." She turned and walked with intentional dignity up the stairs.

"And so you have another piece in this puzzle that surrounds Clifford Hawkins's murder." The sound trailed off behind her as Carrie pulled the door shut, slid the lock into place, and pounded her fist on the cluttered table.

I pull the pearls tight around her neck. Her great brown eyes bulge, her eyeliner smears, her tongue thickens and slime rolls out of her mouth. Pearls pop one by one, fall to the floor. Her head follows, still grinning, and rolls among the pearls.

The phone rang. "I'll get it," Tricia called, racing in from the kitchen with an empty milk glass still in her hand. Carrie reached down and lifted the receiver.

"Hello?" No one who knew her would call before ten.

The voice on the other end was crisp and bright. "Mrs. Rayborn, this is Jeff Kenilworth from the *Oakland Tribune*. I have a couple of questions for you." Carrie replaced the receiver in the cradle, knelt, and unplugged the phone.

"What did you do that for? I'm expecting Twink to call." Tricia pouted, hand on her hip. Carrie walked past her, ran

water into the teakettle, turned on the burner. Tricia
followed, watching balefully. "Are you gonna leave it like
that all day?"

"First let me wake up, and then we'll talk about the
phone. I don't want to deal with that circus. If you want to
stay home today, that's okay, maybe even better. Every
goddamn parasite reporter will be after you."

Tricia nodded, and her body seemed to relax, as though a
burden had been lifted.

"Remember yesterday . . . your message to Twink?"
Carrie was afraid to hear the answer, but she had to believe
completely in her daughter's innocence. No doubts that
would grow in darkness to become an ugly chasm between
them. "What problem did you take care of, Tricia?"

"I was gonna tell you, Momma, but I was so . . . I
mean, I didn't want you to just find them." Tricia walked
away and returned seconds later with a small disk in her
hand. "I don't want to get pregnant," she said quietly.

Carrie was still, too. She realized that her strongest
feeling was one of relief. "Those things aren't a license to
be—"

"Momma, I know. But Twink and I, we really love each
other."

Carrie decided to let the matter sit, at least for the
moment. "All right. We'll talk more about this another
time. Go call Twink, but be sure you unplug the phone
when you're done." Lost in a whirl of concerns, she gulped
her tea and listened to the sounds of the conversation. The
words were indistinct, but it struck her that this could have
been any Tuesday morning phone call between two people
who would later go to school, hang out, do homework. She
drew tiny spirals with her fingernail across the back of the
warm spoon.

There was a giggle from the alcove, some more words,
and then Tricia was standing in the doorway, the corners of
her full mouth upturned.

"He's a riot. He asked me if I would be his bodyguard."

Tricia stands, feet apart, bandillero of bullets across her chest, bayoneted rifle in her hand, stiletto shoved into the top of her high-laced boot. Pilar.

"Hysterical," Carrie said as the phone rang again. She sprang up, shouted "No comment" into the receiver, and slammed it down. "You didn't unplug it like you said you would." She shook the black instrument accusingly at Tricia.

"Sorry, I forgot," Tricia mumbled as she disconnected the phone. Carrie followed her back into the kitchen.

More tea, and toast with peanut butter. The bread in the drawer, peanut butter in the refrigerator. The toaster set to light; if you put it on medium, the toast would burn. Unscrew the lid, get a plate from the drainboard. Get a knife from the ceramic jar above the sink. This isn't going to be easy, Carrie thought, grimly spreading the peanut butter and watching pools of oil rise on the hot bread.

Jay Goldstein lived in San Francisco's Marina district, one of those neighborhoods where joggers had finally outnumbered strollers, especially in the hours just after sunrise and before sunset. After a forty-minute workout in the quiet of his bedroom, Goldstein sat for a while at a morning meditation, clearing his mind and renewing his energy. He enjoyed the short walk to the local bagel and croissant deli off Chestnut Street, where he took his breakfast while watching the bobbing ponytails of the local ladies as they pursued aerobic excellence. He was accustomed to acknowledging three or four passersby, dressed in suits and carrying briefcases, already chewing on the problems of the coming day while he concentrated on spreading the raspberry jam and stirring the double espresso, practicing the credo that anything worth doing should be done with complete attention.

A silver-haired man approached, juggling leather case,

capuccino, and croissant, his neck craning as he searched for a seat. All five tables were occupied, but table sharing was standard practice in this most unmarried of American cities.

"Do you mind?" he asked, pointing with his head to the black wrought-iron chair to Goldstein's right. Without waiting for a response, he dipped his knees, bringing the cup closer to level with the table and eased it out of his hand. He placed the pastry plate to the left of the cup, arranged a white paper napkin on his lap, and smiled. He took a dainty bite of the buttered croissant and returned it to his plate, no signs of crumbs on his fingers. Goldstein examined his own flaky remains, then resumed eating and drinking. The older man leaned forward in his chair, back erect.

"Wonderful, these mild mornings."

"Mm," replied Goldstein, hoping that the intruder had the decency to observe the cardinal rule of table sharing: Conversation must be dropped if the first round is not mutually agreeable.

"My name is Ted Wilson," the man said, as Goldstein peered into his own cup. "I'm here on special assignment. From D.C."

Oh God, thought Goldstein, a government functionary trying to pick me up because he's visiting San Francisco, where he thinks everything goes and everyone swings. "Mm," he replied, gauging the waste involved in leaving half a croissant and some rapidly cooling espresso.

"You're investigating the Hawkins murder, aren't you?"

This in the same tone as the comment on the weather. Jay Goldstein looked up from his coffee. The man's fading tan contrasted nicely with his green eyes and silver hair, his neck was firm, and his tie was YSL. A banker or an attorney? A political crony of his father's?

"Who are you?" asked Goldstein. "Should I know you?"

"Ted Wilson," he said as he set the cup on the saucer in a single motion without fumbling for the indentation, right on target.

"How do you know me?" Goldstein said, watching as a brunette in a blue wool suit and running shoes turned the corner.

"It's my business, Sergeant. Do you think the court was too lenient with Tricia Rayborn?"

"Look, I know that you come from Washington, that you're a very neat eater, and that you know about my job and where I have breakfast. Fine. Now I plan to finish my breakfast and then drive to work. I hope you have somewhere to go, too."

Wilson stirred the remaining foamed milk in the coffee. "I'm a free-lance journalist. I was hoping for your cooperation."

"Sorry, Mr. Wilson, I don't like your tactics," Goldstein said evenly. He took a final look at the cold coffee in his cup, rose, and turned his back on the small black table. A sudden memory, a composite of the countless interviews he had endured when his father was active in Marin County politics, flooded him. Everyone in the family had been schooled in the art of turning attacks to advantage and Jay had learned to enjoy the parry and riposte, but after many years, the excitement had palled. Thank you, Mr. Wilson, he thought, for another dismal flash from the past.

Out of habit, Carlos Cruz turned on the 7:45 local news. It was a signal to Elenya and the boys that breakfast would be ready in five minutes. Juice container in one hand and four folded napkins in the other, he watched a woman on the screen announce that Prince was her best friend and deserved only the finest, real horsemeat. He always wondered about the lady, a dog for a best friend. The picture dissolved to the studio and he set the plastic container in the center of the table and was putting the third napkin under a spoon when he heard her name.

"Tricia Rayborn, seventeen, was found in the car from which the fatal shots that killed young Clifford Hawkins were fired. Our own Lisa Wong is out right now in Oakland with an interview with the Rayborn family." Cut to Fairfax Avenue. Cruz forgot about the toast.

"Morning." Elenya stood between Cruz and the television. "Did you see my folder? It had the new programs I have to turn in for my BASIC class."

"Shh. Hold it a minute." Cruz gently moved her aside and stared at the image on the screen. A bright female voice was speaking.

"And what can you tell us about the Rayborn family, Mrs. Thurmond?"

The camera moved from the smart, alert face of the reporter to an obviously sleepy woman of about fifty, her hair pulled back into a single thin braid from which thinner wisps escaped.

"Well, the mother is a painter, single lady, nice but kind of, you know, well, maybe not so stable."

Carlos Jr. and Julio clattered into the kitchen, bumping into Elenya in the preoccupation of their argument. "Okay, knock it off, you two. Your papa wants to see this," she admonished, separating them and pressing them into their seats. Despite her warning, the boys continued to whisper as Carrie's disembodied voice floated out of the speaker.

"I think things must be pretty slow for both you and the district attorney if the best you can do is innuendos."

"All right!" Cruz grinned. He was hardly aware that he had spoken, and the boys stopped arguing to watch their papa talk to the TV. Lisa Wong's soft features came up close.

"That was Tricia Rayborn's mother, Carrie, a painter who has had several shows at the Tremaine Gallery in San Francisco. And now, back to you, Peter." Once again the studio came up on the screen and Cruz leaned forward and turned the set off.

"Ah, Papa, they didn't do the sports yet. Can I put it back on, please?" Julio pushed back his chair and stood up.

"Yeah," Carlos Jr. added, "they're doing a story about how the Forty-Niners are gonna spend the summer."

"No, let's have some quiet now. And you guys better hustle. It's getting late."

The older boy scowled, poured milk into his bowl, and bent his head to hear the noises. "Was that a case you're working on, Papa?" he asked, hand on the sugar bowl.

"Don't drink your juice so fast, Julio. You'll make your stomach cold." Elenya reached over to slick back a tuft of hair that had sprung up in the center of the boy's part.

"You know I don't talk about my work with you guys. Now, what time is soccer practice today? I'm gonna be very busy. I hope I'm not late."

"Aw, Papa, please don't be late. The other kids get real mad. They say you don't care about the team."

Cruz looked up from his coffee. "And what do you say?"

"I tell them that you're real important and maybe you're on the trail of a dangerous killer and if you stop for a dumb soccer practice, they might be the ones the killer would get the next time." Carlos Jr. beamed with pride.

Cruz winced and hoped that someday they wouldn't think of his work as glamorous. "Now listen, I really want to be the soccer coach. I want to be a good one. Sometimes I can't make it on time because I'm in the middle of an investigation. But I don't want you going around scaring your friends and making such a big deal. It's only a job."

Carlos Jr. and Julio looked at each other as if to say, "Who does he think he's fooling?" and gulped down the last of their orange juice. They jumped up at the same instant.

"Oh shit, it's eight o'clock," Carlos Jr. yelled.

"Carlos Cruz Jr., you come back here," Elenya said.

"How many times do I have to tell you that such language is not acceptable in this family?" She glowered.

"But Papa always says it when—"

"A ten-year-old boy listens to his mama and his papa, and his mama and his papa have told him not to use that language, right?"

The boy lowered his head. "Sorry, Mama."

"Okay. Just go now and be more careful of what you say. Go on." She waved him out of the room with her napkin. "I saw that something bothered you about that interview. What was it?"

Cruz thought that she hadn't noticed. "I don't know. They carry it too far, coming into someone's life just when they're in trouble. And the real ugly part is that the audience eats it up, along with their toast and eggs. It's not right." He brushed a pile of crumbs into a mound in front of him.

Elenya started clearing the table, stacking bowls together. She passed his chair and kissed the top of his head. "I love you, *querido*, but you can't fix everything." He looked into her eyes. "You know, you really should try to make it to the game on time today."

"I'll make it, don't worry. I have a three o'clock meeting with the captain, but I'll be done in time for practice."

He felt lighter. Breakfast with Elenya and the boys could last him until midafternoon, unless something came along to mess up that good warm feeling.

# 8

Goldstein and Morella sat on opposite sides of the otherwise empty room, eyes on the papers in front of them. The coffee and bagel brigade had blown in and then back out again, and Ted Wilson's crumbless breakfast invasion hung over Goldstein like an uninvited poltergeist, sitting on his shoulder and prodding him with questions. Where did the man plan to send his article? *Mother Jones? Atlantic Monthly? True Detective Tales?* Was Wilson one of those journalists with a mission? Improve the quality of life, see justice done, moral imperatives. Bring the world a step closer to utopia.

Goldstein's mouth fell open and he felt a chill of comprehension blow over him. Utopia. Oneida. The boarding house. He reached for the telephone book, flipped through the pages to the heading OBERMAN-OSGOOD, and ran his finger down the second column. There it was. Oneida West Development Corporation. No address, just a telephone number with a San Francisco exchange. He dialed and drummed on the desk, remembering his American Concepts 1 reading list: Thoreau and Melville, Emerson and the Transcendentalists. Oneida was one of those mid-nineteenth century experiments that attempted to create a perfect society. Communal living and high ideals. A man answered.

"Oneida West. Can we help you?"

Goldstein shifted into Nasal Bureaucratic. "Yessir. This is Mr. Nietzsche. Berkeley Pacific Gas and Electric office. There seems to be a problem. We haven't received a payment from one of your properties for the past two months."

"That can't be. We always pay all our bills promptly." The man was indignant. "There must be an error somewhere."

"Perhaps an incorrect address was entered in our computer. New system, you know."

The man snorted into the phone.

"Be patient, sir. We're trying to get things worked out. Now, just tell me—is one of your properties located at 1505 Shattuck?" Goldstein asked, bringing the maps into clear focus in his mind, visualizing the yellow line that ran through Berkeley.

"Now, how in the world did you get that? Our house is at 1722 Vine."

"Well, that explains everything. We'll have this rectified in no time, sir. Sorry to bother you." Solicitous. Not too apologetic.

"And now I suppose you're going to turn off the power until we pay. I know how you people work." More indignation.

"Oh no, sir," Goldstein said. "You can just forget about those bills." And he hung up, smiling.

The address was too far from Oakland to say that he hadn't realized he was out of his jurisdiction. He should call, enlist the cooperation of the Berkeley police, but he knew he wouldn't. Morella stared at him, amused.

"Neechee, huh? Where did you get that name from? You're beginning to act like a television show, Goldstein. Pretty soon you'll even have a blond secretary with a heart of gold and big bazooms."

"We do what we have to, Morella," Goldstein answered

with a diffident shrug. "The name just came to me. Old friend of the family." Family—did the Rayborn family have anything to do with Oneida? "I have some stops to make. If Cruz checks in, tell him that I'll meet him at the Golden Dragon at noon, and it's his turn to buy."

Morella perked up. "They got good eggrolls? I haven't had a really great eggroll in weeks. They're either too greasy or else they're all shredded *cabbage*, for chrissake." He reached into his pocket and extracted a five-dollar bill. "Hey, bring me a couple, okay?"

"Sure, Morella. How many do you want?"

"As many as this will buy. Can't tell until I've had at least two or three whether I like them or not."

The house was third from the corner, set a few feet farther back than the others, a rambling accretion of rooms that appeared to have been stuck on whenever more space was needed. The entire structure had been covered over by a layer of redwood shingles in an attempt to disguise the piecemeal additions. A broad pine towered over the approach, forcing the flagstone path to jog to the right to go around its girth. On the steps, arms folded across his chest, stood a man with a full red beard, looking like a chewing tobacco ad sprung to life.

"Are you looking for someone?" he demanded.

"Good morning. My name's Schopenhauer. City Housing Authority. I have official business with the manager of this building."

"I'm the manager. What's the problem?" The man's bulk filled the doorway.

"I am afraid we have received reports of violations. To save our agency and yourself possible embarrassment, this is a courtesy call, shall we say." Goldstein kept his hands folded in front of him, feet apart, like a football player in a lineup. "We can go over them point by point and perhaps get them cleared up before the official visit."

"What official visit?" the man asked, small plucking motions of his fingers the only visible sign of his concern.

"Oh, didn't you get the notice? Next Wednesday. But if we can take care of things now, then there's no problem." Goldstein watched sternly while the man continued to stare and pluck.

"Okay, but I'm in a hurry. I have a meeting in San Francisco." He turned, and Goldstein followed him into the house.

"Sorry, I didn't get your name," Goldstein said as he glanced around the living room. Tweed couch, vinyl chairs, a table; *Starry Night* on one wall, *A View from Toledo* on the other.

"Ian MacPherson. What's the problem, anyway?"

"Well now, Mr. MacPherson. Point one. This area is zoned for a maximum of three unrelated persons in the same dwelling, unless specifically licensed. I could find no license on file, and it has been reported that there are six people living here."

MacPherson frowned and tugged on his beard. "That's your mistake. We got a license eleven months ago. Sounds like a mess-up to me. Typical," he said, the last word escaping in a whisper.

Not very friendly, thought Goldstein, but at least he isn't always licking his chops like Khamir.

"Well, I'll just have to check again. If you locate your copy by Wednesday, that would help. Now, point two. And this is the more serious problem, I hope you realize, Mr. MacPherson. Point Two. A complaint has been filed stating that you are manufacturing something here, that there is machinery going all day. This is, as you know, strictly against ordinance ten-sixty-six, section twelve." This is more fun than I thought it would be, Goldstein thought.

"Wait a minute. This is just a boarding house. Who filed that complaint anyway?" The color rose on MacPherson's cheeks and his eyes narrowed in challenge.

"That is confidential," Goldstein said, wagging his finger. "I can't violate the anonymity of the filer, but as the filee you are certainly entitled to disprove the claim." His tone became graver, soothing. "Why don't we just walk through the rooms? If I visually verify what you say, I will inform the inspector, and he may not find it necessary to repeat this next week."

"All right, but let's be quick about it. I can't be late. You'll see for yourself that there's nothing to see."

Goldstein walked behind MacPherson, first upstairs through a succession of spotless bedrooms, then downstairs to a small laundry room, a kitchen that was so sanitary it showed no signs of food preparation, and a dining room. The dining room wallpaper was a busy little Jacobean reproduction and he noted that they had had the good sense not to hang anything else on the walls. Not even maps.

"Look," MacPherson said. "This is absurd. There's no machinery here. We have a television, a radio, and a vacuum cleaner. Maybe that's it. Maybe someone heard the vacuum cleaner."

They walked back into the hall. "Sometimes," Goldstein offered, "these complaints come from some unfortunate person who has nothing else to do. I still have to investigate. But from the look of things, you can rest assured that there will be no visit from the inspector." Goldstein hid his disappointment with a smile. At least he didn't have to tell anyone about this. It could pass mercifully into oblivion, unshared. He started toward the door. "You wouldn't happen to have machinery hidden in this broom closet, would you?" he asked, raising his eyebrows as he rested his hand on the chrome knob. The color drained from MacPherson's face and he coughed.

"Oh, that's not a broom closet. It's just a small reading room with bookshelves and a chair. Not big enough for equipment of any sort." Goldstein's warning lights, primed since his encounter with Ted Wilson, flashed on.

"Now let's just hold it for a minute. You told me we'd seen all the downstairs rooms and now you say there's one I haven't seen. Well, of course I'm going to have to let the inspector know. Who knows what other violations *he* might find." He sounded righteous and felt expectant.

MacPherson sighed. "All right, look," he said, pushing the door open. "Just a reading room, see?"

Goldstein peered past him at a row of shelves and an old green club chair. "Sorry, but I must actually be in the room." MacPherson stepped aside and Goldstein entered the tiny room, went to the shelves, then turned to go out. The maps were on the other wall. The yellow lines were identical to the ones on Khamir's map. His breathing quickened and he clamped his teeth together with the effort of keeping still.

"Thanks. Well, the inspector should be satisfied now." They walked to the front door together and MacPherson paused to lock it behind him.

"What did you say your name was?" he asked.

"Uh, Spinoza. Fred Spinoza."

"Well, I hope I won't be bothered with this again, Mr. Spinoza." They continued past the pine.

"No need to worry. Have a nice day, Mr. MacPherson." Goldstein waved and waited for MacPherson to make a right turn onto the street, then walked off in the opposite direction. He didn't want to arouse MacPherson's interest in him. At least not yet.

The campanile stood in the center of the university campus. In the 1970s, the Berkeley bell tower had been called an energy sink and people swore that they were mysteriously drawn to it. Now it was, once again, simply a landmark. For Jay Goldstein, it was the likeliest place to run into Mother, a skinny black man who had somehow managed to sustain the spirit of the Weathermen and Panthers while advocating a high-fiber diet and weekly hot tubs as the keys to health. Mother had been one of the first to transport the message of revolution to the Stanford campus in 1969, where Jay had actually entered into his dialogue, offering vigorous arguments in favor of using the system itself to eradicate its own injustices. Those exchanges earned him a place of affection in Mother's heart, which Jay, as a policeman, cultivated for the day when it could be turned to his professional advantage. Mother was one of a select handful who could stir Goldstein's intellectual juices and have him asking whether it was the premise or the logic that led to the untenable conclusion.

If he waited long enough, he was sure that Mother's loping stride and trademark Afro, now flecked with gray, would come into view. The sun was warm and it was comfortable to sit and let the events of the morning and the days before come up and entertain him. Maps. Multinational rooming houses. Carrie Rayborn's long fingers around the water cup. Arabs and bagels and a blood-soaked porch.

The entire campus is a magnet, he mused, as he searched for Mother in the late morning crowd. Radical middle-aged women in tennis shoes with battered Samuel Gompers tracts in their bookbags. Boys in glasses, slide rules replaced now by multifunction calculators. Girls with angora sweaters and pink lipstick. Men with earrings, women in ties and suits. Winos, social workers, football players, Rastas, even an occasional boy from Iowa. All ingredients in the Berkeley soup. But where was Mother? Goldstein looked at his watch; perhaps this was an indulgence.

Pushing his way through the group that had gathered for the midday speeches around Sproul Hall, he walked toward Sather Gate, scanning the throng for Mother. He passed the announcement boards without reading them and headed for the street. Four carts, gypsy wagons selling Middle Eastern fast food, lined the sidewalk to the left of the campus exit, and there in front of the one nearest to Goldstein stood Mother, munching on a stuffed pita bread.

"*Que pasa*, babe?" Mother said, grinning and chewing at the same time. "How's business?"

"You know how it goes," Goldstein answered with his own smile. "One little crisis is all it takes to keep things stirred up."

"Hey, Mother," chirped a tiny blonde with braids and Birkenstocks flapping as she went by, "I'm finished with your book."

He swiveled his head as she passed. "Bring it back then, baby. The whole rest of the world needs educating." He bit into the sandwich, shredded lettuce dripping from his mouth.

"Come by tonight and get it, why doncha?" the girl said.

"Some things never change." Mother winked as the girl walked away. "She wants all sorts of education. Never learned nothing useful in Michigan."

"And you're just the guy to help her out, right?" Goldstein had watched variations on the scene scores of times in the sixteen years they had known each other. Mother was still as concerned for the erudition of young women as he had always been.

"You here for business, pleasure, or learning?" Mother asked.

"You get around, and I need some information that might help me keep a seventeen-year-old girl from taking a murder rap."

Mother's eyes widened and he smiled. "You gonna introduce me? She need educating?"

"She needs something else right now." He didn't want to make a show of his urgency. Mother's interest would be most aroused if Goldstein fed him only small bits of the story. "Do you know anything about a group that has rooming houses in Berkeley, Oakland, San Francisco, all over? They only take in young men with different cultural backgrounds."

"Hey, if you said they were all young women, you know

I'd have the answer. But young men—. . . doesn't ring a bell." They walked down the street toward the Orange Julius stand, and a thin boy in a Che beret raised his fist in salute to Mother as he passed. The tall man pursed his pink lips. "Tell me more."

"Does the name 'Oneida' mean anything to you?" They waited for a break in the traffic. Streams of people flowed by, several stopping to greet Mother.

"Like in silverware?" Mother asked. "My people were into all that capitalist decadence, you know. I didn't even have the advantage of growing up in the slums. Had to come by my revolutionary ways through other means." He paused. "Naw, don't mean shit to me."

Goldstein led the way to a storefront and ordered two large drinks. He waited while the blenders whirred, took the tall containers, and walked out onto the teeming street again.

"Do me a favor. Ask around for me, anything about a group called Oneida, boarding houses with blacks, Orientals, Chicanos, Europeans. I can't tell you why, and I don't want you to use my name, but it could be important for one young girl." Goldstein twirled his straw.

"Hey, wait a minute," Mother said, one eye closing as the other eyebrow shot up. "Is this group maybe some new movement? You asking me to turn in brothers and sisters?"

"I'm not interested in their politics," Goldstein said, shaking his head. "But they seem to think they can go around killing people. That's bound to have an effect on your basic law enforcement agencies. They'll start to look at everyone except Democrats and Republicans as danger-ous."

"You're not out to destroy the bearers of the latest message?" Mother asked, slurping the last drops of the orange drink noisily.

"Just doing my job," Goldstein answered, extending his

hand. "If you hear anything, call this number and leave a message. I'd appreciate it."

Mother grasped his hand and grinned. "Hey, wanna get beaten at chess?"

"Sure. It's gotten boring. I can't seem to lose anymore, since we stopped playing. But not today."

Mother walked away smiling. When Goldstein turned, Mother had his arm around a tall girl, almost as thin and black as he, who was wearing pink pumps, white stockings, and a pink suit.

# 9

"Aw, c'mon, Mr. Cruz, do I hafta play on this side? I can't see nothing 'cause of the sun." To prove his point, the boy raised his hand to his forehead, looking up at Cruz through shielded eyes.

"Danny, when we play against Frank's Hardware next week, we'll be out on the field at four-thirty, just like now, and half the time the sun will be in your eyes and the rest of the time it will be in their eyes. So just practice following the ball. Watch it all the time. Now get back in there and show me what you can do." Cruz clapped his hands and the team took positions on the patchy green and brown of the playing field. Danny waited with the others for Cruz to blow the whistle, and made a show of squinting and rubbing his eyes.

"Okay," Cruz shouted, "I want the halfbacks to remember to pass to the forwards. And let's try for some goals from further away. And stick to your man. Ready?"

A chorus of voices yelled back that they were ready.

Cruz blew his whistle and an explosion of arms and legs raced toward the visitor's goal, propelling the ball ahead of them. The pack skidded to a stop, pivoted, and ran in the opposite direction as the ball was stolen by the other side. Corinda, the second oldest on the team after Carlos Jr. and a head taller than the others, danced the ball into position and kicked hard. The goalie lunged, missed, and lay in the dirt, pounding his fist into the ground.

"Jerry, don't get so carried away. Everyone misses once in a while," Cruz said. "You're doing great."

Jerry brushed himself off, straightened his knee pads, and retrieved the ball, his freckled face grim with disappointment. He kicked the ball off to the left, intending Julio to receive, but it was picked off by Becky, who bounced it off her right knee.

"Keep up with her, Danny. Watch the ball," Cruz shouted. Corinda leaped into the air, pointed a beautiful header, and landed on one foot, the other already stretched behind her ready to kick into forward motion. Julio, Gail, Sean, and Nathan surged ahead, scrambling over the uneven surface of the grass in a tangle. Danny trailed behind, making desultory progress in the direction of the action as he assessed the angle of the sun. The rest of the team was nearly at the end of the field as Sean slammed the ball with the side of his foot. Shrieks of victory turned to moans as the goalie batted the ball away, and the play moved back toward the middle of the field.

Cruz wished that he could be out there, running and screaming—it would be a good remedy for the long and frustrating day he had suffered. How useless to spend a morning with an old lady who didn't have the strength to sit up straight, never mind pull the trigger and withstand the recoil of a 30.06 rifle. How stupid to spend an afternoon trying to track down a pathetic little desk clerk who had had the bad fortune to have been beaten by Clifford Hawkins and the good fortune to have had his presence at the seedy hotel Sunday night attested to by several co-workers and a guest. Just his luck that this case would be one that Goldstein was in charge of. The last one had been his, according to the department policy of partners alternating lead positions, an ordinary Mama-shoots-Papa that was wrapped up in three hours, triplicates and all.

"Hey, Danny, watch out!" Carlos Jr. yelled from the other end of the field. Cruz looked up to see Corinda, full tilt, smash into Danny, who immediately fell to the ground gasping and clutching his stomach. Cruz trotted out to the circle of players gathered around the fallen boy.

"Okay, take five," he said, bending over Danny, who by now had a greenish cast to his face. "Where does it hurt, Danny?" he asked, looking to see if any limbs were askew.

"My stomach," the boy wailed, "I think she broke my stomach."

"Stomachs don't break, Danny. You got the wind knocked out of you, that's all." Cruz put his arm under the boy's head. "Now, take deep breaths and count to sixty. You'll feel better in a minute."

"Need any help?" The voice was familiar. Cruz looked up, but it took him several seconds to recognize Royal Kerner out of the context of his grandmother's house.

"Got the wind knocked out of him. He'll be all right in a minute."

"Hey, you'll be fine," Royal said, kneeling beside Cruz and Danny. "If you want to hard enough, you can get up and start playing again. You ever hear of Nietzsche?" he said, patting the stack of books he had been carrying. Danny stared up at him. "He says that people are at their best when they show a strength of will. You know what that means?" Danny shook his head. "It means you can do whatever needs to be done, if you believe in yourself."

"What brings you around here?" Cruz asked, helping Danny to a sitting position.

"I wanted to talk to you and you said you coached soccer down here, so I came by. Do you have a minute?"

Cruz looked back down at Danny, who was up to twenty-seven and counting aloud, a good sign that he was recovering from the blow. "Sure," he said, standing up. "Keep counting, Danny." The rest of the team sat panting and giggling behind the goal, passing oranges and cans of apple juice around. Corinda brought an orange to Danny, who sat up, held out his hand, and went on counting. Cruz followed Royal to the lone bench, near the sideline at midfield.

"Well, what can I do for you?" Cruz asked, watching as Danny accepted Corinda's peace offering.

"I thought you should know that . . . uh, I wanted to tell you about Clifford Hawkins." He ran his finger along the spine of the thickest book.

Cruz turned slightly so that he was looking straight at the boy. Why did he wait until now, he wondered, when he could have told me whatever it was yesterday?

"You have information about his death?" Cruz asked.

"I think you should understand about Hawkins. He was the dark side of man. Did you ever read *Faust* or the original *Dr. Jekyll and Mr. Hyde*?" Cruz shook his head. "Hawkins hurt a lot of people. He only took on the vulnerable ones, you know what I mean? People who weren't up to the challenge of his evil. That little girl, do you know about her?"

Cruz nodded his head. "Your grandmother told me about her. Annie Marsten, right?"

Royal didn't answer. "And Jimmy Jackson, that hotel clerk Hawkins hurt so badly?"

"Thanks for your trouble, coming out here and everything, Royal. We're checking with those people already."

"What about Charlie Hernandez? Charlie and Paco."

"Who?" said Cruz. The team was starting to break up into twos and threes, some talking quietly, others kicking the empty juice cans aimlessly near the goal.

"Charlie was handicapped, had to walk with arm braces because his legs were so weak," Royal said. Beneath the glasses, his eyes were sad and angry, both at the same time. "But you know, all the people in the neighborhood, they encouraged him, treated him like a real person. Except for Hawkins. Hawkins used to tease Charlie, once even knocked his braces out from under him. Paco is Charlie's older brother, and he got so angry, he smashed Hawkins, right in the face. But it didn't do any good. Hawkins just got him one night, beat him really bad. Do you know why people do things like that, Sergeant?"

Cruz shook his head. "Who knows? Maybe he had a hard childhood."

"My dad died when I was nine and my mother worked in a factory, double shifts when she could, to keep us together. I did all the cleaning and cooking, looked after Jess and Thomas. Lots of people don't have it easy," Royal said as he pushed his glasses back up to the bridge of his nose and sat lost in his own thoughts, his expression solemn. "You know what I think?" he added. "I think Clifford Hawkins was an incarnation of pure evil."

At the far end of the field, Ted and a smaller boy began to shout, and Ted threw up his hands in mock defeat. As he walked away, the smaller boy gave Ted a shove that sent him to his knees. "All right, you two. If you get into a fight, I'll kick you both off the team. Go sit down." Cruz massaged his neck, dropped his head, and let it hang as he rubbed the muscles between his shoulders.

"Is that what you wanted to tell me, Royal? I only have another fifteen minutes with these kids. Have to get them home by five." He was tired, the kids were getting impatient, and Royal was telling him stuff he already knew.

"Do you agree with Kant when he talks about man's innate moral sense? I mean, if that's true, then how do people like Clifford Hawkins get to be the way they are? Listen to this." Royal leafed through the fattest of the books, stopping twice and nodding his head in apparent agreement with what he was reading. "Here, in *Critique of Pure Reason*, he says—"

"I'm sorry, Royal. I really have to get back to the kids. Maybe you should talk to my partner. He studied philosophy; he'd know all that stuff. I majored in sociology, you know what I mean?'' Cruz gave two sharp blasts on his whistle and the team tossed their cans down and rushed to the middle of the field. "All right, go back there and pick up that trash and put it where it belongs," he shouted. "You're using up practice time now."

Grumbling and shoving, the children ran back and collected the cans and orange peels, tossed them into an overflowing wire basket, and hurried to the field.

"These kids should have more of a sense of responsibility," Royal said, fixing his books into a neat package. "Well, I have to get home and study." He shifted his books to his other arm and walked toward the sidewalk.

Thanks for the information on Hernandez, but if you came to give me advice, Cruz thought, I'm not interested. He blew the whistle again. "Practice is over," he shouted.

# 10

"I knew it. As soon as I read the paper, I knew that you would be missing sleep, not eating properly, not paying attention to your body's signals."

Carrie was unwilling to let Marty go through his clucking tonight for much longer. She was tired, and the tension had finally been replaced by a pleasant softness in her muscles. She and Tricia had spent the day together, phone unplugged and doorbell unanswered. They had had tuna sandwiches on the back porch and listened to Rampal play Telemann. Once, Tricia brought up the subject of her upcoming trial, and once Carrie asked Tricia why she had stolen the car. It had been a struggle not to rage at the girl, but she wanted to give Tricia her support, not her anger. It made Carrie feel better, too.

"Sometimes, Marty, I don't think about my body for days."

Marty's hands shaped a beachball-sized space and he smiled at Carrie. "But all tasks are easier, all thinking clearer if the machinery is kept in the best condition." He leaned back into the pillow on the daybed and propped his feet on the small table.

"Hey, look, go easy on that sprouts and whales stuff with me tonight," Carrie said. "I almost didn't let you in when the bell rang. I thought you were another goddamn reporter. It's been a zoo here all day."

Marty squeezed Carrie's upper arm. "I thought your energy paths could use a rest and you did say Tuesday night, so I came anyway. We should look at the tape; it'll take your mind off things, give your feeling centers a chance to heal and get ready for the next round of stresses."

Carrie glared at him and he shrugged his shoulders and turned his palms up helplessly.

"How long is the tape?" Carrie asked. She decided that if it was any longer than seven minutes, she would tell him not tonight, she'd changed her mind.

"Eight minutes and eleven seconds. Unedited."

"All right," she agreed, "but then I need some sleep."

Marty inserted the cassette. It whirred to a starting position and he held down the pause button.

"I want you to pay attention to the lighting. There are these incredible halos around some of the paintings, like I captured their auras. And you look—well, really exciting, a strong woman image, kind of like a Hopi princess." He beamed at her.

"Hopis didn't have princesses. They didn't have kings or queens, either," Carrie said impatiently.

"Well, if they'd had them, you'd look like one," Marty said, not giving up. "But if it makes you feel any better, let's just say that you look like a powerful, beautiful female magician."

"So. I look witchy," Carrie teased.

"Never. You are the soul of sorcery, a fountain of mystery, a source."

"Oh, is that all?" she asked, groaning at the responsibility. "Okay, let's get this over with."

Marty grimaced at her, then started the videotape. The first shot was a sweep of the studio, the wall of storage, neat shelves with linseed oil, tubes of cerulean, cobalt, cerise, magenta, mauve, maroon. Jars of brushes, palette knives, a pile of newsprint, rolls of unstretched canvas, folded rags. Then the compartmented stacking system for the drawings, some of them twenty years old, an archive of Carrie's emerging vision. She shuddered at the memory of how close she had come, three times, to tearing them all up, shredding the evidence. In the end, she had sensed that they were the only connections, besides Tricia, that held her to a tangible past; she had chosen not to be adrift.

"How about a little Vivaldi here, to show the duality of passion and precision at work?" Marty suggested.

"I lent my Vivaldi to Linda. The whole collection," Carrie answered, twisting her feet under her and pulling down the cotton skirt.

"I don't mean now, wise guy. As a sound-over for the finished product."

Okay, so he's not a total airhead, she thought. "Sure, good, that works." She still felt an eerie detachment from the images on the small screen. The film was good, his framing selective, and the music would be fine. She waited to see herself. He had tried for a long time to get her to agree to do the taping; she had stage fright, she felt awkward, she didn't want to see all the tiny age lines around her eyes, she should really clean up the studio and wash the windows first. But finally she had agreed, and after an hour of moving about and preparing, the painting itself took over; she hadn't known exactly when it was that Marty began taping.

There she was. The Carrie on the screen moved surely, sipping from the china cup, then picking up the broad flat brush and stepping into the magic circle that surrounded the canvas and sucked her in whenever she got close enough. The painting was one of the larger ones, and Marty had been clever, she admitted, showing small areas, emphasizing the gestural nature of her work.

The camera pulled back to a long shot. Hair looks pretty nice, all Hepburn knot and wisps, Carrie thought, feeling better and better.

"I like this more than I thought I would," she said pleasantly.

"Thanks a whole lot. Why did you do it if you didn't think it would be any good?"

"That's not what I meant," Carrie said as Tricia came into the room.

"Hi, Marty," the girl said. "That's pretty good." She pointed in the direction of the screen.

"Thanks, kiddo. I've been sending you positive thoughts, you know. I just wanted to tell you that I know it's going to be okay for you. It will all work out the way it's supposed to." ·

"Yeah, sure. What if I'm supposed to get screwed and go to jail for the rest of my life?"

"No, no, that isn't the way it is. You're good, and good will come to you if you open yourself to it," he said gravely.

"Stop that thing, will you?" Carrie asked Marty. She turned to Tricia. "Do you want to watch this with us?"

"Well, actually, I was gonna ask you if I could call Twink. Just to talk for a while. And I promise I won't forget to unplug it this time," she added as she bent down beside the table and reconnected the telephone.

"Okay, but take it in the kitchen, please. This only has a few more minutes to run. I want to see the whole thing and then I'm going to bed."

White china cup, amber tea, and amber brandy. Ivory sheets tight against the mattress. Creamy satin pajamas with blue piping and C.R. scrolled on the pocket. Carved cherubs on a brass lamp, pleated shade, pull chain.

The telephone rang.

"Oh shit," Carrie yelled, "don't they ever give up! Goddamn vultures. Let me get it," she ordered, reaching out for Tricia to pass her the phone. "Yes," she shouted into the receiver. There was a long silence; Carrie was aware of Marty and Tricia, standing next to each other and staring at her.

"Yes, that's true but I don't see your point." More silence. Carrie tapped her foot, carried the phone with her as she walked into the studio, stood in front of the new canvas shaking her head, paced back into the alcove, looked up at Tricia and then away.

"But, Mr. Morrisey, that's totally unjustified." Tricia's smile faded. Carrie nodded into the phone, took a deep breath, and said, "Goddamn self-serving uptight bastard," and slammed the receiver down.

"He fired me. Oh, he didn't put it that way. Said maybe I shouldn't come in to the office for a while until things get straightened out. For my own good. Said the publicity was hurting his business, but that he was really concerned about me." Carrie pounded her fist on the table, tears coming to her eyes. She shouldn't let Tricia see her like this. She should be strong, a refuge. But the anger was alive now— anger at Mr. Morrisey, certainly, but also at Tricia; she had, after all, really stolen the car, really lied to her about where she was that night, really screwed up royally.

"That's not so terrible, Momma. You've been saying for months that you hate that job and that you're getting out as soon as you have the chance. So now you have the chance." She put her arms around Carrie, but Carrie couldn't return the hug. "You want me to get you a drink or something?"

Get it together, Carrie warned herself. Think about something good.

"No. Wait, yes, a brandy," Carrie said. "Thanks, Trish. I'm really sorry for that display." Carrie felt some of the stiffness drain from her body, and she took Tricia's hand. "We'll be okay. We'll make it."

Marty wandered absently back into the alcove. "Thought you ladies could use a little refreshment," he said, holding three glasses of brandy. Carrie reached for the fullest one

and Marty passed one to Tricia. "To new beginnings." He
held his glass high.

"And to occasional periods of coasting," Carrie added.
Tricia frowned, as though they were both speaking in
tongues, and swallowed the brandy in two gulps. She
shuddered. Carrie and Marty both watched, astonished.

"Well," said Marty, setting down his glass, "I guess we
can see the rest of this some other time. I think I'll leave you
two alone now. There are only a couple of shots left
anyway." He kissed Carrie's cheek.

"Wait." She turned her face away. "Why don't we all
watch the tape together? I don't want to think, not yet." Her
arms felt warm. The brandy was working. "You want to see
your mother, the unemployed star?" Carrie asked, holding
up Marty's glass to ask if he wanted a refill.

"Sure," Tricia said, "but don't expect rave reviews from
me. The only movies I ever really liked were *The Great
Escape* and *My Bodyguard*." She smiled graciously.

"You never know," Marty said. "You might be witness-
ing the birth of the next Robert Altman."

"Who?" Tricia asked.

"Never mind, just watch the masterpiece." Marty started
the tape. Carrie and Tricia sat beside each other.

"Hey, this is better than I thought it would be," Tricia
said.

"Did you two rehearse?" Marty asked.

"What do you mean?" Tricia took Marty's glass from his
hand and finished the remaining half inch of brandy.

"*Stop!*" Carrie shouted. She flew from her seat to the
television, shot through with enormous, unexpected energy.
"Did you see it?"

"You mean where the colors go a little too green? I know.
I need a new lens filter."

"*No!* The dog. Stop the tape, Marty."

"Dog?" Tricia said, staring at Carrie.

"Marty, stop the goddamn tape." What was it that the

woman in the red shirt had said? Something about a poodle with black around its eyes. And the big guy, the one with the beer belly, had agreed. Now, here in the living room, was a white, curly-haired dog, a poodle looking for all the world like it was wearing two black eye patches.

"Oh shit, this is perfect," Carrie said, lighting a cigarette and exhaling a cloud of smoke.

"Yeah, I thought it was pretty good. Contrast between the abstract act of making a painting and the everyday squalor of the street," Marty said.

Carrie didn't answer. She was staring at the image on the screen; the dog on a leash was stopping to sniff a pile in the grass. Another second and the person on the other end of the leash would stroll into the camera's field. Tricia would be safe.

"Oh, Tricia, this is terrific. Don't you see what this means?" she demanded, turning toward Marty. "I want to isolate him on the screen. I'll set up my camera and if I get a hold of Larry, I'll have him make up some five-by-sevens to take to Goldstein and Cruz. Then all they have to do is find the owner. Maybe Larry is still working. Where did I put his number?" Her face was warm and she went to the kitchen, spilled some brandy into her glass, and returned.

"Whoa, slow down a little, lady," Marty said. "Cruz and Goldstein don't live at the precinct. You need some rest. You should know you can't keep your body going on brandy and cigarettes during a trauma like this. At least, take some B vitamins."

"I don't know what either one of you is talking about. You're both nuts." Tricia hugged her stomach and stepped back, away from Carrie and Marty.

"I'll explain in a second. I just have to see the next shot on the tape," Carrie said, pressing the start button. She sat forward, concentrating on the lower right-hand quadrant of the small screen. The dog was still sniffing, not going anywhere. The camera panned left, then faded; there was the back of her own head again, the painting, the inside of her studio.

"Why didn't you get him?" Carrie started to tremble and Marty backed away.

"Don't break my machine. Please," Marty said.

"You edited this tape, didn't you? Cut the murderer right out," Carrie said through her teeth.

"Can't you act like a normal person? Why don't you just stop this dumb game? I can't stand it," Tricia screamed. She stomped through the kitchen into the hall and slammed her door.

Carrie sank onto the sofa, white and shaking. "Let me keep the tape for tonight, okay? I'm gonna get some good pictures of the dog anyway."

Marty drew a deep breath and his shoulders fell. He knelt on the floor, not touching her. "Carrie, where is this all going to get you? You can't accuse a dog of murder."

"Look," she replied as if she were talking to a dim-witted six-year-old, "this dog was in that car when Hawkins was killed, and it wasn't there when Tricia stole the car."

"So what?" he said, touching her knee. "I don't see your point."

"The dog has an owner and I'll bet the owner was in the car," Carrie said, searching his eyes for affirmation. "And I bet the owner lives around here because you generally walk your dog near where you live, right?" She pulled away from Marty's touch. "So all I have to do is get a good still photograph of the dog, take it to Goldstein, and he'll find the owner." She shook her hair back and started for the kitchen. Marty didn't follow her.

"Maybe," he called, as she poured another brandy.

"What do you mean, 'maybe?' It's so logical."

"Look," he said, "I'm tired and I have a big shoot tomorrow, so I better go. Keep the tape; take pictures of the dog. God knows, I hope you're right." He stood up and went to the door. "Keep yourself open to the good things."

# PART

# 4

# WEDNESDAY

# 11

Carrie held the contact sheet in front of her and squinted. Some of the tiny pictures were of the canvas she was currently working on, one was of Tricia clowning in the garden, and the rest were of the dog on Marty's videotape. She had selected three for enlargement. She checked the red light above Larry's door; he wasn't finished yet. Goldstein and Cruz said they would be at the station at 12:30, so there was still more than an hour left. She heard the water running in the darkroom; at least five more minutes before she could see the prints. She should have asked Larry what kind of paper he'd be using, she thought. Perhaps the print would be grainy or lacking contrast. Shit, this isn't an art show, she reminded herself.

> The milling crowd murmurs and points, plastic wine-glasses in hand. They ooze past the framed display. Black and white photographs. The poodle in profile. Chiaroscuro poodle. A bird's-eye view of the poodle. The poodle in a Diane Arbus tutu, walking down an aisle.

That's how painters make money, she thought. Cater to the public tastes, whatever they happen to be this week. Make images that are bizarre or pretty. And now that I don't have a job, goddamn Morrisey all the way to his lawn party, the time may be right for me to tap into the money source, and let go of all this truth-and-beauty crap.

Six minutes had passed since the water stopped running. She wanted to look out a window, watch mothers pushing babies in strollers, look at kids on skateboards, see old ladies with their mysterious packages, but there was no window. She knocked on the darkroom door.

"Hey, can I come in? You almost done?" she called.

"Two more minutes. Why don't you look at that folder marked 'Transformations'? Take your mind off the waiting," Larry said through the door, his voice muffled, low.

She picked up the top folder on the counter, flipped through a series of photographs of the same man at different stages of his life, from back-to-nature youthfulness through a succession of jobs to an apparently worldly and satisfied entrepreneurial smugness. He changed with the times, she thought, he prospered, but was he happy? Am I happy? Maybe it's time to find out what sells and make paintings that make money. She was relieved when the door opened and Larry emerged from the darkroom.

"Okay, sweets, here are the prints and here are your negatives. I'm not sure if it's going to work," he said, "but good luck anyway."

"Thanks, Larry."

"Hey, what did you think of the pictures?" he asked, tapping the folder.

"Interesting, Larry. They're truly interesting."

The large man at the corner desk examined a piece of bagel, then popped it into his mouth.

"Yes, ma'am, can I help you?" he asked, chewing and talking at the same time.

"Yes, I'm here to see Sergeant Goldstein." Carrie suddenly felt expansive and gracious.

"Sergeant Goldstein isn't in," the man said. "I think his partner's somewhere around, though."

"Hi," said Cruz, stepping into the office. "This is Sergeant Morella." Morella nodded, still chewing. "And this is Mrs. Rayborn."

Carrie smiled again. "Can we talk someplace?" She clutched the envelope to her chest. "This won't take very long."

"Do you mind talking here?" Cruz asked. "Someone else is using the interview room, and we'd have to go down to the cafeteria. Sergeant Goldstein should be back any second and I don't want to miss him."

The planes of his face catch the light. Shadows pool under his cheekbones, his blue eyes fill with indigo. His lips form a round space, then close into a stretched oval as he speaks into the receiver.

"No, that's fine," Carrie said, filled with goodwill and affection. He was going to help her. "Here," she said, setting the envelope on his desk.

His eyebrows drew together as he unwound the string from the two paper disks, opened the flap, and pulled out three photographs, spreading them in front of him. "This is a dog, Mrs. Rayborn. Are you sure you brought the right pictures?" he asked slowly.

"This is the dog that was with whoever killed Clifford Hawkins. In the car with him. I had it enlarged from a videotape."

Cruz coughed, and his face turned red. "I don't think I understand."

Step by step, Carrie explained, getting all the threads of her hypothesis to run in the same direction. She told him everything, from the overheard conversations in the street, to her conviction that Tricia was telling the truth, to her first viewing of the tape. Cruz was silent.

"So when we find the owner of the dog, we'll have the killer and your daughter will be free," he said, looking quickly over to Morella's desk. Carrie saw the man, one of his chins resting in his folded hands, watching them intently.

"Well, there are still charges she'll have to face," Carrie said. "But murder won't be one of them."

"Mrs. Rayborn," Cruz began, "even if a dog was in the car, and even if this really is a picture of that dog, and even if we do find it, that wouldn't prove that Tricia didn't kill Hawkins. She could have picked the dog up off the street, just like she picked up Angela."

Pricks of heat ran along Carrie's cheeks. Her breathing quickened and she dug her fingernails into the palms of her hands. She counted to eight and let clean air fill her chest and move up into her head. The light was suffused with white, the red washed away.

"I don't want to lie to you, Mrs. Rayborn." Cruz leaned forward as if to divulge a confidence. "Don't get your hopes too high."

"Will you follow this up or not?" Carrie said coldly.

"Follow what up?" the voice behind her asked. Goldstein walked around to the other side of the desk and picked up the top print of the dog, holding it by the corner. "Good afternoon, Mrs. Rayborn. What's this, Carlos?"

"I think Mrs. Rayborn can explain it better than I can," Cruz said.

Carrie waited as Goldstein bent over the photographs, his blond hair falling softly toward his forehead. Then she told the story again, finishing with the request that they show the photos around the neighborhood and try to locate the dog and its owner.

Goldstein's eyes locked into hers as she ended her speech. A chill proceeded from the inside of her chest out to her skin. He didn't believe her either. Is it all fantasy? she wondered. No, she decided, heart beating again, this is right; it has to work.

"What are you going to do?" Carrie asked, looking at Goldstein and ignoring Cruz.

"We'll make some inquiries, Mrs. Rayborn," Goldstein answered. "But don't exaggerate the importance of these photographs. It's just too early to know. Why don't you go home and try to get some rest? You look like you could use some sleep," he said. "Maybe vitamins would help."

Another one, Carrie thought. I don't need two of them.

"You just take care of the murderer and I'll take care of the rest of my life," she said as she moved off into the dark hall.

# 12

Cruz searched the nameplates beside the six doorbells. No Hernandez, but one bell had no name, and he pressed the buzzer next to it. No answer. He tried the bell below. A buzz sounded, and he pushed open the glass door. Radio chatter and a television game show blared from an apartment on the ground floor. A voice from upstairs called, "T.J., that you?"

Cruz's eyes, now accustomed to the lack of light, looked up at a woman wearing white shorts, a pink tube top, and hair curlers. She frowned and pulled her head inside. The door banged closed just as Cruz reached the top of the stairs.

"Whoever you are, go away. Get out of this building." Her voice was shrill.

"I'm Sergeant Cruz, Oakland Police Department," he said to the closed door.

"Yeah, sure, and maybe next time you'll be taking a survey about deodorant soap. Go away."

"Look, just open the door enough for me to show you my shield. This won't take very long."

"No way. You leave now before I call the real police."

Occasionally, an interview with a closed door between the questions and the answers was the only way to get what he needed. "Okay, don't open the door. Just listen for a minute." There was a silence.

"So?" the voice behind the door said.

"I'm trying to find the Hernandez family. The last known address is this building."

"What do you want to know for?"

"Do they have a small white poodle with black patches on both eyes? I'm looking for the dog."

"What'd he do, stick up a bank?" She laughed. "We can't have pets here. Landlord throws you out if you do."

"Does the Hernandez family live here, ma'am?"

"Not anymore. They took those kids and their noisy electric guitars and moved out. Just yesterday."

"Shit," Cruz said, his mind racing. Maybe Carrie Rayborn was on to something. Maybe the landlord had discovered that the Hernandez boys had a dog, and forced them to move. Maybe Paco Hernandez had extracted final payment for all the pain Hawkins inflicted on the disabled boy.

"What? I couldn't hear you."

"I just asked if you know where they moved to?"

"Not my business. As long as it's plenty far from me."

Cruz scribbled in his pad, flipped it closed, and said, "You've been great. Thanks for your cooperation."

The next name was Marsten. The little girl who had been assaulted by Hawkins in the alley. Cruz's stomach did an acrobatic flip. No complaint had ever been filed, and he was willing to bet that the little girl hadn't been seen by a counselor. Secret shame. Silent suffering. Maybe he could at least offer them the name of the therapist the department recommended; the girl would be affected in any case, but it was a question of more or less damage now. The address was two blocks away and he walked slowly, hoping that his stomach would stop churning.

It was no use. His body refused to get the message. He was suddenly very thirsty, and the grocery store was just a few steps away. The store was dark, and smells of cheese and spilled milk mingled with fresh apple scents. Mrs.

Llobante waved to him, as if he were an old customer who stopped in every day. He went to the soda case, slid open the glass door, and pulled out a Coke, pressing the metal flip-top back and taking a long drink. It hit his throat, slid down easily, and then stopped in a big bubble just below his breastbone.

The tiny woman, half hidden by the cash register, watched as he laid five dimes on the counter. "It goes well?" she asked.

In response, he handed her the picture of the dog. She leaned on one elbow, looked at the photograph, then at Cruz.

"You selling him?" she asked, interested.

"No, no. Have you ever seen this dog, Mrs. Llobante?" Cruz said.

She narrowed her eyes. "No dogs allowed in here." She pointed to a hand-lettered sign beside the door.

"I just thought you might have seen this dog at some time," Cruz said. "You must see everything in this neighborhood."

She smiled at the acknowledgment. "Yes, I do see everything, but not this dog."

Cruz was about to return the print to the folder when the door swung open again and Royal Kerner came in.

"Hello, Royal. How's school?"

"Two tests tomorrow. Lots of work," he said. He picked out a loaf of whole wheat bread and walked to the counter. Cruz held the photograph above the flap of the envelope. Why not? he thought. He laid the picture on the counter, next to Royal's bread.

"Did you ever see this dog?" Cruz said.

Royal stared at the print, bread dangling from his hand. "Why do you ask?"

"It's a long story. Have you ever seen him?"

"Can't say that I have," Royal said. He put three quarters and two pennies in Mrs. Llobante's hand, grabbed the puckered plastic end of the bread bag, and walked quickly away from the counter.

"Hey, you wanna bag for that bread?" Mrs. Llobante called as the doors swung closed behind the boy.

"Guess he didn't hear you," Cruz said. "He doesn't live around here anyway. Must think I'm crazy, asking about a dog." He slipped the photograph back into the envelope, left his empty Coke can on the counter, and walked back out onto the street, just in time to catch Royal's compact body turn up the walk to the Franklin house.

Cruz crossed the street, quickening his pace as he neared the Marsten address, and half hoped that no one would be home, but there on the front step, just beyond a patch of lawn that was already dry and brown, a woman with pale skin and pale hair struggled with grocery bags that were in imminent danger of spilling open. She juggled them into position so that she could reach into her pocket, pulled out a key, and opened the door.

Cruz bounded up the steps. "Here, let me help you."

The woman's face lit up with momentary gratitude, quickly replaced by a sorrowful stare. She clutched her bags tighter and clung to the woven purse that hung from her shoulder.

"Sorry to frighten you. I'm Sergeant Cruz, Oakland Police Department," he explained, showing his badge. She quietly handed him a paper sack and walked straight back into the kitchen.

He waited until she had deposited the bags on the counter and then showed her the photograph. Mrs. Marsten removed her fingers from the collar of her sweater and sighed, as if in thanks that this was all that was expected of her. She held the picture daintily, two fingers on the upper corner, and brought it closer. There was little change in her expression, only a deepening line on her forehead as she concentrated.

"There are lots of dogs on this street, but it's not one of those than runs around every day." The woman paused, her eyes downcast. "Our lawn, Sergeant Cruz, they all come up on the grass and"—she stared at the floor—"soil it."

"So you don't think you've ever seen this dog?" he asked again, not ready to talk about Hawkins and Annie.

"Wait a minute. You know, I think maybe I have seen this dog, but it wasn't here. It isn't one of them that comes up on the lawn. I remember all of them, spend half my life keeping other people's dogs off my grass, but once dogs have picked a place, they keep coming back to it, you see." She took cans and boxes out of the paper bags. "I saw that dog, oh, about two months ago. I remember because it was Easter Sunday, and me and Jack and Annie were on our way back from church. Annie stopped to pet the dog. It was on a leash and there was this girl, all dressed in her fine clothes, and the dog was wearing a pink bow."

This is ridiculous, thought Cruz. How am I going to go from talking about poodles to child molesters?

"Who was the girl, Mrs. Marsten?" he asked, stalling.

She shook her head. "I've seen her once or twice. About my height, near high school age, I guess, black. But see, we've only lived here since January. Came out from Oklahoma. My husband is a typesetter, thought he could get a better job here." She rubbed at a scratch on the countertop absentmindedly. "So far, all he can find is night work. Security guard is all."

Cruz was ready now. "Mrs. Marsten, I have two reasons for being here. I wanted to ask you about the dog, and also about what happened between your daughter and Clifford Hawkins."

She set two containers of milk, a package of cheese, and a pound of butter on the counter next to the refrigerator. She reached into the bag and got out a can of tomato soup, a box of Minute Rice, and three potatoes. She kept her back to Cruz, and went on taking things out of the bags and putting them on the counter, as though he had never asked about her daughter.

"Mrs. Marsten," Cruz said. When she turned around,

Cruz saw her face, wet with tears. She made no sound, turned around again, and began to set more cans and boxes on shelves. He waited.

"You don't know . . . it's so bad. There's no one to talk to about it. My husband, he gets so mad if I say anything. And Annie." She shook her head as she picked up a box of Rice Krispies. "Why, Sergeant? How can people do such things?"

Cruz walked around the yellow counter, stood close to her without touching her. "I'm sorry, Mrs. Marsten. Maybe there's something I can do to help."

"She sits in a corner in school and won't play with the other children anymore. She wears her oldest clothes all the time. There are scratches all over her arms and legs. She says the cat did it, but I saw her the other day digging her nails into her arm until it bled. When I try to talk to her she won't even look at me." The woman stopped crying. "I'm glad he's dead. He can't do this to any more children, but it's too late for my Annie."

Cruz felt sick; his stomach again. "Annie needs help. She has to know that it wasn't her fault." He swallowed and the nausea receded. "Here's a number you can call, a counselor who can help Annie. And you," he said as he slid a piece of paper toward her. The woman didn't pick it up.

"How can anyone help? It's too late," she whispered.

"No, Mrs. Marsten. Annie has the whole rest of her life to live, and these people know how to work with children who have . . . who are confused and afraid about what happened to them."

"I don't know, Sergeant. Why can't they figure out how to help before it happens, before more little girls are hurt by people like Clifford Hawkins?"

Cruz had no answer.

# 13

"It's not that I don't trust you personally, babe. You and me, we go back a long way. But you gotta remember. It's different now and I'm not gonna lay anything on you without getting something back." Mother's face gleamed with droplets of salty mist. He swung his arm in a large arc at the restaurants and shops that overlooked the water and said, "See, this place is just one example. Pretty, right? All this money spent to prettify a place that only the lawyers and computer people can afford to go to, when it could have been more docks, more jobs for poor people. That's why I can't give you something for nothing. Too long, we've been giving it away too long."

They walked past a small marina with sailboats and cabin cruisers rocking in their berths, the sound of the water lapping against the pier boards like an irregular heartbeat. A gull swooped down, grabbed a piece of something soft and brown from the water, and soared off again to a moss-covered post, where it consumed its feast in solitary pleasure.

"Come on, Mother, we both know it's not so simple. That's another argument for another day. Right now, I need all the help I can get."

"And so does Ashika," Mother said, stopping in front of a menu taped to the window of a restaurant. "She's in jail, her bail is out of sight, and you can help her." He shaded his eyes and pressed his nose to the glass. Just like a kid in a pastry shop, Goldstein thought. Give everyone enough dimes and there would be no revolution.

"All right," Goldstein said, walking to a weathered bench, "tell me about her. It goes against my higher principles to make deals but maybe something can be worked out."

"Well, Mr. Philosopher," Mother said, his eyes large in mock surprise. "Morality goes out the window when it's not expedient, eh?" There was none of the camaraderie that Goldstein was accustomed to; now, there was only challenge.

"Well," Goldstein said softly, "sometimes the ends justify the means. It's this damn relativity problem I have. Concrete rules don't always apply." He shook his head at the dilemma he had hoped to solve by becoming a philosophy teacher years ago. The duality: the absolute offered comfort, the relative offered freedom, and he didn't think they could coexist.

"You tell me about Ashika," Goldstein said, following the creaking sound below to an old Monterey fishing boat that bumped into the dock as the water rose and fell, "and I'll think about it. I'll call you tomorrow with my answer. Deal or no deal." He walked over to the railing, leaned his hands on the splintery top bar, and stared across the bay to the Erector-Set gridwork of the shipyards. "But I need some proof that you know enough about Oneida to make the deal worth it." Mother uncrossed his long legs and broke into a grin that showed all his fine teeth. Goldstein wondered if they were capped.

"Okay, first the proof. This is as much as you get until I have your answer." Mother picked up a stone and rolled it in his fingers. "You know about my calling as a teacher, right?" Goldstein smiled. Mother had lovingly cultivated the impression that he was merely a lecher in revolutionary clothing. "I ran into one of my students the other day. Now follow me, all right, friend?" he said, turning his face toward Goldstein's. "She got the message, so to speak, and been studying, trying to figure things out, so she takes herself to the OneWorld Bookstore in San Francisco, to pick up some new reading material. Well, she meets a lad there who talks to her, they leave together, and, being young and healthy, they want to sleep together. But the lad says 'Sorry, I can't take you home. I live in a boarding house and we can't have female guests. In fact,' the lad says, 'we aren't even supposed to have female friends.' So she takes him to a place she knows. It's Saturday and the physics lab at Berkeley is unoccupied, and they go back there and find momentary paradise. And after, the lad tells her about this Oneida, and says that he has changed his mind, he wants out, and he tells her all about it. And she tells me all about it. And I tell you all about it, if you spring Ashika."

Goldstein watched the man's face during the speech. After countless games of chess and scores of evenings drinking coffee and talking, he was sure he knew some of Mother's tricks, but this appeared to be genuine truth-telling, and his only source of information about Oneida so far. Was the death of Clifford Hawkins an example of what happens when the faithful attempt to leave Oneida? Was this boy afraid he would suffer the same fate?

"Maybe we can make a deal," Goldstein said. "Now tell me why Ashika is in jail."

"I don't think it has a name, but they're calling it embezzlement. She used to work for one of the big banks as a computer operator in the mortgage processing department. When the interest rates shot up, she started to see a lot of people, mostly in the poorer neighborhoods, losing their homes. They had those damn fool adjustable mortgages, and when interest rates went up, so did their payments. But their wages never changed, right? So she made it look like they had paid up. Made the computer tell the reports that no more delinquencies were occurring." His chest swelled with pride. "She didn't steal anything. She never got anything out of it personally, but it was her way of seeing justice done. She learned good from old Mother." His smile reflected genuine delight. "So all I'm asking is that you figure out a way to get the D.A. to have the judge reduce her bail from fifty thousand to something more reasonable like, say five thousand."

"How come her bail is so high?" Goldstein asked. "If she doesn't have access to the computer anymore and she didn't commit a violent crime or have a record, then it is excessive."

Mother looked at the stone in his hand. "They found out that she was living with Lewis Muhamdar. Said that she might take advantage and disappear."

"That does make it more difficult, you know," Goldstein said. "Muhamdar has a national reputation for advocating violence, and even though it's argumentum ad hominem, I can't sail into the district attorney's office and tell him to reduce her bail because maybe I'll get some third-hand information from a source whose reliability we can't even check. I mean, that's from his point of view, and I'd have to give him something more. If I decide it's worth it to deal at all."

Mother threw the stone into the oily water below and watched it sink next to a spiffy cabin cruiser.

"I'll call you tomorrow," Goldstein said, "and let you know what I've decided. But I want you to reconsider your position. Think about a seventeen-year-old girl spending years in jail. And try to live up to Rousseau's expectations." He let the sentence hang as he followed the progress of an oil tanker moving slowly toward the open waters of the bay. Feel for her, Goldstein thought. They don't call you Mother for nothing.

"Well, babe, ain't you gonna tell me? My head is full of

so much that I can't remember what every single fey philosopher said."

Goldstein laughed. "He believed that man was essentially good. I'm counting on your goodness."

Mother's eyelids fluttered and he bowed. "You call me tonight. My little girl from the bookstore is coming by around nine. She says she has to get some of the facts right. Says this bunch is about to launch into some new phase, and her boyfriend wants out before things get any heavier." Mother walked toward the roadway and Goldstein followed, half a step behind.

"Maybe there's something else I can do for you instead of Ashika," Goldstein said. "That may be a little beyond my power. Think about it. I'm willing to give you something in exchange for what you know, but don't ask me for something I can't deliver."

"Call me tonight," Mother said, waving and walking to the other side of the street. Goldstein watched him for a block or two and finally lost him in the crowd at the bus-stop.

The sun took its time burning off the morning fog, and it was midafternoon before the sky was completely free of overcast. And in another two hours it will all come rolling in again, Goldstein thought, as he headed up the rocky path. He had taken the long drive to the Marin County side of the Golden Gate Bridge to look at the bunkers that were plainly one of the critical points on Oneida's maps. Wind blew across the hill, pushing back the fog, which swirled in great upswept drafts to lick at the red clay cliffs above the water. From atop one of the concrete slabs, he watched a container ship slide under the bridge and his mind was quiet. He was eyes and ears and skin, and he delighted in the clean feeling, damp and chill, as the wind poured over him.

But his brain chatter resumed after a short time. There was too much going on in the Hawkins case and, so far, none of it was behaving properly. Intractable data, his logic teacher used to call it, and he had learned to recognize that particular obstacle when he ran into it. The only remedy was to slow down, wait for another piece to appear, and then sort out what was relevant and what was in the way.

He smiled at the thought of Mother's girls; so easy for some people, direct and uncomplicated, but for him always full of reservations and qualifications. He had learned that he could, at the same time, be attracted to someone and still do things that were nearly guaranteed to send them away. He liked Carrie Rayborn. Under other circumstances, her restless hands and small rounded belly, her long, rebellious hair, and her green eyes would have excited him. And he would have made contact successfully, and they would have made love, and afterward, he would have said something hurtful. Maybe about her childishness in thinking that she could make a living as a painter, or something about her sense of personal style, relaxed, funky, a statement. So, better not begin what could only end badly. With regret, he turned back to the BMW. Time to find out what Oneida meant to Tricia Rayborn.

He drove across the Richmond Bridge at San Rafael, avoiding the traffic of downtown San Francisco, and let his mind drift with the counterpoint of a Bach prelude. He arrived at Fairfax Avenue with no memory of the freeway or the streets that he had just been on.

He rang the bell and stepped back into the street to give Carrie a chance to see who it was, but the answering buzz came at once and he pushed against the door hurriedly. At the second-floor landing he knocked and called, "Hello?" Light footsteps sounded, feet sliding the last yard to the door. Tricia Rayborn, surprised, stood in front of him.

"Oh, hi," she said, leaning one elbow against the wood as she stuck her left foot on her right. "What now?" Her eyes were wide and her cheeks pink.

"Relax, Tricia. I'm not here to take you away. I just have

a few more questions." He listened for sounds of someone else in the apartment.

"Yeah, so go ahead." Tricia's breathing slowed and her pupils contracted. "My mother's not home; went to pick up some new canvases this guy was stretching for her," she said, as if to explain why they were talking in the hall instead of the privacy of the flat.

"Can I come in?" Goldstein asked. "I don't think it's such a good idea to have all the neighbors hear what we have to say," he added, pointing his head in the direction of the other doors.

Tricia stepped aside and they went into the kitchen. She opened the refrigerator, bent over, and pulled a stalk of celery out of the vegetable bin. She looks a lot like her mother, Goldstein thought, only she's not as tall and her short hair and narrow hips are almost androgynous.

"I'm sorry, I didn't hear you," he said. Tricia was standing in front of him with her head cocked, a quizzical look on her face.

"I said, do you want some celery?"

"No, thanks. Let's just get the business over with. What do you know about the Transcendentalists?" he asked.

A slow smile spread across her face. "Did my mother get you to ask me that? She's been trying to get me to learn that transcendental meditation stuff for years, but I think it's all a bunch of crap," she said, still amused, and a took a large crunching bite of the celery.

Test #1—pass. "This has nothing to do with your mother or with transcendental meditation," Goldstein said, watching for a change, some hooding of her eyes, a turning away of her head. The side of her cheek bulged squirrellike, and she moved her jaw up and down and rolled the food to the other side of her mouth.

"So what does it have to do with?" she asked, swallowing.

"Let me ask the questions, Tricia. Does the name

'Oneida' mean anything to you?" he asked. No change in her eyes.

"Sounds like frozen french fries," she said with a giggle. "I don't know, guess I never heard of him."

Either she was a proficient liar, Goldstein thought, or there really was no connection between Tricia Rayborn and Oneida. Then, if Hawkins's erratic, antisocial behavior had become a threat to the group and they got rid of him, where did Tricia and the car fit in? Maybe someone from the group gave her the car, to create confusion. Or maybe the shots had been timed to look like they came from the car. This was not neat.

"Tricia, do you know anyone from 1228?"

"I already told you and those other guys Sunday night. I know the Chinese guy to say hello to, but I don't even know his name. They're a bunch of weirdos, if you ask me. Clifford I kinda knew because of all the shit he was giving Charlie Hernandez. We were trying to figure out how to get him to stop being so mean to Charlie." She stopped talking and her chest rose and fell rapidly. She stared at Goldstein. This was the first time that he had seen her show real fear. What had she said that made her afraid? And how could he use the fear?

"Well, he's not bothering Charlie anymore, is he?" Goldstein said, no hint of humor on his face. "Problem solved, right, Tricia?" The girl was now sliding both her hands back and forth across the edge of the table, and her eyes followed her fingers. "Was it a group decision, Tricia, or did you figure out that the way to stop Hawkins from bothering Charlie was to kill him?" He waited. "Maybe you didn't think about it, but when John Kim Soong offered you the car, you took it, and then he told you there was a gun in the car, and went over all the things Hawkins had done, and you both agreed that Hawkins was a mess, dangerous, and you were going to take care of it." Now he got up and stood in front of Tricia, adding physical intimidation to the already threatening reality of his power.

"Maybe you were tricked into taking the car, and someone else was sitting next to you and fired the gun that killed Hawkins, and you're not talking because he told you that the law would hold you just as responsible, so you developed a story that is so thin it melts, and you think you're protected. I've got news for you. You're not."

Tricia sobbed and, without warning, had her arms around him, pressing her body to his. This is not a genderless human being, he thought.

"I'm scared," she said between muffled sobs.

Jay Goldstein reached up, pulled her arms away, and stepped back. "That's an old trick, Tricia, but it won't work with me. Sure you're scared, but if you didn't kill Hawkins, then the only thing that will help you is to tell the truth."

"You bastard," she hissed. "I wasn't playing a game with you. I was just afraid and alone, and you seemed to be a human being. I should've fucking known better." She stomped to the table and sat with a thud in the chair that Goldstein had vacated. Two patches of red rose from her neck.

Feeling assaulted himself, Goldstein took a tentative step toward the table. Maybe he had overdone it. He put a hand on her arm and she looked up, eyes flaming with anger and lips pursed closed.

"It's my job, Tricia," he said. Her mouth softened into the beginning of a cautious smile. "I have to go now. If you think of anything, call me. Anytime." He handed her a card. "That's my home phone and my address, in case you can't get me at the station."

What a balancing act, he thought. Go too far in one direction, compensate, then wait. Equilibrium would probably be boring, anyway.

# PART

# 5

# THURSDAY

# 14

The counteroffer that he had been prepared to make had gone untendered. Goldstein had dialed Mother's number, without success, every half hour between 8 P.M. and midnight. A search for Mother could range from Berkeley to San Francisco, from Oakland to Palo Alto. Goldstein had slept fitfully, awakening with thoughts of Oneida scrambling for his attention, even before he was fully conscious. He cut his usual forty-minute workout to fifteen minutes, anxious to see what the meditation would bring. His teacher, a wrinkled old man named Yamasake, had left him with a final caveat: Don't presume to look, he had said. The truth will find you.

Oneida: he felt an exhilaration, like the excitement he had known after reading Hegel's "Absolute Idea" for the third time, knowing that on the next reading, he would unlock its secrets. In all the other areas of his life, he remained recognizable to himself; it was the quiver of anticipation whenever he thought about Oneida that was different. He had become both participant and observer, and the paradox had blurred crucial lines of demarcation.

Cruz had tactfully remarked that maybe Goldstein should slow down a little, but he couldn't help himself, and besides, he didn't want to.

Using the name Santayana, Goldstein called the Oneida

office. He had been hired to give estimates on paint jobs for
the houses in San Francisco, San Rafael, and San Mateo,
but had lost the addresses, he said. After a short pause, the
weary voice read off the information and hung up without
saying good-bye.

He only half listened as Cruz explained that Mrs. Marsten
had indeed seen someone with the dog but that she didn't
know who the girl was. It made sense, he said. If the dog
appeared on the tape, then it had been on the street and so
why shouldn't someone have seen it? He argued that there
was, right now, enough circumstantial evidence to arrest
Tricia Rayborn. Goldstein reminded him that the district
attorney had flatly refused to issue a warrant unless there
was either a weapon or a witness.

Cruz waved grumpily when Goldstein left for the Oneida
house on Fairfax. He wanted them to be aware of his
interest—maybe one of the young men would make a
mistake, or come forward, seeking protection.

All the window shades but one were drawn down to the
sills. A space of four inches had been left below the shade in
the far right window, and Goldstein bent down and looked
in. Four men sat around the dining room table with their
backs to the window. He could see the bottoms of their
sweaters and a slice of someone's knees, standing in front of
the others. The standing figure was speaking, and judging
from his height and the leanness of his legs, it was either
Khamir or Soong. He couldn't make out any words, only
the rhythmic rise and fall of the voice. The lecturer stepped
back, raised a wooden pointer, and angled his body slightly.
Goldstein envisioned the dark little man pointing at the red
circles on the map that had been removed on the morning of
his second visit.

He crouched lower, changing his perspective and willing
the speaker to talk louder. It was Khamir and he was
pointing to the map, but something new had been added.

From each of the red circles, a yellow arrow pointed toward the mouth of the bay. Whatever was going on inside was not meant to be seen by an Oakland detective, he was certain.

The four seated men rose. One voice began, the cadence clipped and regular, and the same rhythms were repeated by the others, all just out of range of clear audibility.

He picked up a few words—"restore" and "sacrifice" and "mandate," he thought, but nothing was coherent. Impatient with the scattered information, he rang the bell. There was a flurry of footsteps and the sound of furniture being moved. He rang again.

"Yes, who's there?" the unmistakable voice asked.

"It's Detective Goldstein, Mr. Khamir."

The door opened and Khamir, in brown corduroy pants, smiled at him. "Come in. What can I do for you?" His tongue licked at his mustache.

"Oh, a few more questions, that's all." Goldstein looked into the dining room. Empty. Through the other arch, the four young boarders sat in the living room talking softly. Pretty little domestic scene, thought Goldstein, all brotherhood and tranquility. "I see everyone's still home. Nice that you could all arrange to be together."

Khamir's eyes turned a shade blacker. "No, my dear Detective Goldstein. It just happened that today, we all had a bit of free time, so I took advantage of the situation to ask the men if they knew of anyone who was looking for a room, since we have a vacancy." He smiled disarmingly, mustache gleaming with moisture. The others sat planted, not looking up, embodiments of innocence. Jay Goldstein wasn't ready to disturb them. Not quite yet.

"Speaking of that vacancy, Mr. Khamir, do you know where Clifford Hawkins was going when he was murdered?"

"Now, Sergeant Goldstein, I have told you before that I was out at the time, at a meeting. I don't have the least idea what that unfortunate young man was doing or where he was going." Khamir's lower lip retreated behind his teeth.

"Well, then, I think I'll ask the others," Goldstein said.

Khamir's left eye twitched. "Certainly. I have to get the papers I need for my meeting." Noiselessly, as though he had no weight or substance, he moved down the hall. *They are the hollow men,* Goldstein thought. T. S. Eliot must have been inspired by this bunch when he wrote that. There was an emptiness about all these people, nothing behind their eyes, a robotic quality to their humorless, literal speech.

"Good morning, gentlemen," he said. Eight eyes looked up and four mouths said hello. "I have some questions. Do any of you know where Clifford Hawkins was going when he left the house Sunday night?" He looked at Miguel Santos and John Soong. Santos put his hands in his lap and swallowed, his throat muscles moving visibly. Soong turned in his chair and said that all he knew was that Hawkins was on his way out.

"I don't have the slightest idea where he was going. He didn't talk much to anyone around here," Soong added, "after he started getting into trouble."

Seeing them all together made Goldstein's skin prickle. All those crew neck sweaters and corduroy pants, such an incongruous lot. He could almost hear them waiting, without the volition to move until some secret signal freed them. Goldstein waited with them.

"By the way, I was wondering if any of you have any theories about what led to all those changes in Hawkins's behavior?" No one spoke for several seconds.

Soong shifted in his chair again and fiddled with his watch. "He just changed," he said. "We tried to help him, but in the end, he didn't want any help."


"What time did he call?" Goldstein asked. The phone booth on the corner of MacArthur Boulevard was noisy.

Trucks and cars, exhaust systems in disrepair, clogged the streets.

"Ten minutes ago," Cruz said. "He said it was urgent. Said to say thank you for taking care of things so fast, and that he was prepared to keep his end of the bargain. Said to meet at the usual place between nine and ten this morning. It's nine-forty-five now, man. You better hustle."

Goldstein hung up and walked to his car. Evidently, Ashika had been sprung, and Mother believed that Goldstein had arranged it. Gentleman that he was, Mother would be true to his pledge. Far be it for me, Goldstein thought, to relieve him of the notion that he owes me something. How sweet it would be if things were right or wrong, black or white, yes or no. But it had never been that way for him, never would be, at least not while life insisted on presenting him with the ability to see several layers at once. He drove to the Berkeley campus, parked in the underground lot on Bowditch, and walked to the falafel wagons. Mother wasn't there.

Goldstein tried Sather Gate and the plaza in front of Sproul Hall. He was ten minutes late; he had missed Mother. He had to find out what the man had learned about Oneida. What big action did they have planned? Why couldn't someone say, "Aw gee, fellas, I don't feel like playing anymore"? The answer, he was sure, would explain Hawkins's murder and not incidentally save any others who changed their minds and wanted out. But he needed Mother's pieces to complete the puzzle.

Reluctantly, he gave a final glance around the campus entrance. Maybe Mother was in one of the cafés or bookstores on Telegraph, catching up on the local news. Goldstein checked three coffeehouses. Little time machines, he thought, as he stood outside of Cody's bookstore. Overwhelming noise levels. Espresso machines and tables full of men in berets and sandals, engaged in loud conversation with women wearing black sweaters and no makeup.

Mother would contact him again, hopefully before he discovered that Goldstein had nothing to do with the release of Ashika.

The search for Mother continued in his mind as he started the engine and backed out of the cramped parking space, avoiding contact with the pole on his left and the Volvo on his right. He pulled up at the exit to the street and stopped to let three girls cross in front of him. Easing the car onto Bowditch, he turned left, and waited for a break in the traffic on the corner of Bancroft, watching the sidewalks for Mother.

There he was, his back to the street, talking to a girl with spiked hair and six earrings. Goldstein pulled to the curb and rolled down the window.

"Sorry I was late," he shouted.

"Hey, *que pasa,* babe?" Mother said. He patted the girl on the back, then ambled over to the car, opened the passenger door, and got in. "Just so happens I need a ride to Oakland. I got to talk to Ashika," he said, smiling broadly.

"Just so happens, I'm going that way," Goldstein said. "You sure don't give a person much margin." He drove off into the street traffic, swinging wide around the double-parked cars.

"Hey, babe, you know, I didn't think you'd do it. Took some right thinking on your part, and I want to congratulate you. You just bought yourself some good kharma, not to mention what I'm about to tell you."

"What did you find out about Oneida?" Goldstein asked.

"Let's do this civilized. Observe the niceties. If we don't have that, then what is there?" Mother's voice was light, teasing, and Goldstein forced his body to relax. "Okay, you passed all the tests. I get bored when things are easy and this was too easy. It's not right to amuse myself at your expense, so here it is." He took out a pack of Gauloises and lit one, returning the blue pack to his shirt pocket.

"At least open the window," Goldstein said. "Those things smell like singed feathers."

Mother rolled the window down. "Oneida is a collection of kids recruited on the streets and at unemployment offices, places like that. They feel like they bought into the American dream only to find that, for them, it's more like a nightmare. I coulda told them, if they asked Mother." He tossed the cigarette out the open window. "Vile. Anyway, they believed the promises of wealth and brotherhood and were a bit put out to find that there is still prejudice and poverty. I coulda saved them the disappointment."

"So that explains the cultural diversity of the group," Goldstein said, choosing his words carefully. "But so far, it all sounds like what you've been saying since these kids were in kindergarten. What's different about Oneida?"

"Well now, here's the good part," Mother said. "And believe me, there's more to know than the little girl told me, more than her boyfriend knows. I tell you, she was scared, her old white face got paler and paler, and she doesn't know all that much. About four sentences' worth."

"So what are they? The four sentences, I mean," Goldstein said.

"I'm getting there. There was some subtle stuff, too, you know. Reading between the lines makes me tired."

Goldstein raised an eyebrow; Mother had always been a good observer, and could be relied on to burrow down to the heart of a situation. "Sorry. Take your time," he conceded.

"Okay, babe. This Oneida wants to reestablish the principles this country was founded on. You know, equal opportunity, no discrimination, democratic decision-making, and all that rah-rah. They're training a cadre of troops in New York, Chicago, Washington, Miami, L.A., Dallas, here. Think they're going to do a Nicaraguan-style takeover. They got some maneuvers coming up to see how well the troops take orders and shake out the bugs for the big one. And they don't take kindly to people who want to leave. And that's the four sentences, babe." Mother shifted his long legs and laughed.

"How many people, altogether?" Goldstein asked, his mind racing with questions, plans, strategies. "Can they really do anything?"

"No way, babe. About fifty, a hundred people each city. Only thing they can do is hurt whoever happens to be in their way, you know. The city poor. No power behind the words, you know what I mean? That's the wrong way to do it."

"Do what?" Goldstein asked.

"Hey, real revolution comes from teaching, from spreading the word and letting the people choose the way, so that it really belongs to them. That's the only way to make it stick, you know. From the hearts of the people."

"Okay, put the political theory on hold for now. What's the girl's name? Maybe she can answer some of my questions, turn me on to her boyfriend. We could work something out."

"Tsk-tsk, there you go. Lost your manners again. I promised her I wouldn't tell her name," Mother said, "and that's the only reason she told me what she knows."

"All right, listen. We can offer the boy protection, since he wants out anyway."

"I'll tell her about your offer," Mother said. "She might be interested. I'll call you."

Goldstein nodded in agreement.

"You a little slow today," Mother said. Goldstein looked down at the speedometer. Fifty-five. "Slow on the uptake, babe. These here test maneuvers. They're going to happen soon. I don't know when. She just said soon. And the real stuff is going to happen on the Fourth of July."

"What do you mean, she doesn't know when? There are a million people out there, and you tell me some lunatic

bunch is planning to take over the country and to have
so-called test maneuvers soon.''

"Don't get so excited. I'm working on it. Like you said
the other day, I don't want your buddies to start seeing
terrorists behind every black and brown face that walks
down the street. I got my own stake in this.''

"Sorry, but I can't do it that way," Goldstein said. "I
have to call in Intelligence and the Feds.''

"Listen, babe, your collective brainpower and shiny
technology didn't find out about these dudes, Mother did.
Let Mother take care of it." He smiled. "I'll see if I can get
the boy to talk to me. I'll give him your message. I'll be in
touch.''

Goldstein dropped Mother on Grand Avenue, near the
green and blue of Lake Merritt, and then drove downtown.
He'd be talking to Intelligence and the FBI all night, if he
didn't get started now.

# 15

Carrie came awake in pieces. First her legs moved her to the kitchen, where her hands took the teapot to the sink, filled it with water, and set it on the stove. She looked at the clock. Almost eleven. After one cup of tea, her right eye opened and by the time the second cup was finished, her left eye followed. She leaned forward into the heat of her third cup of tea and pulled the green turtleneck closer to her chin.

"Hey, Momma, I was just thinking. How old was I when I got my first two-wheeler?" Tricia dumped a spoonful of sugar into a bowl of cornflakes and poured milk over it.

"How old? Two-wheeler?" Carrie repeated, making sure that she was at least attacking the right problem.

"Yeah, you once told me that I was nine, but that can't be right because when I was nine, we were on Middle Farm with Frankie. I remember my bike when we had the house on President Street, in Brooklyn, when Isaac was living with us, so I must have been about seven." She resumed her race with the cornflakes. Carrie, disconcerted by Frankie's name, didn't answer. He had been a surprise. When they moved from Brooklyn to Hillsdale, about a hundred miles north of the city, Carrie was seeking peace and a return to natural rhythms. Instead, she found a farmer, whose sweet sexy body helped her forget the loneliness created by Isaac's departure.

"Well, was I seven or nine?" Tricia demanded.

"Nine." Carrie decided she needed more tea.

"No, it couldn't have been. I remember riding with Isaac in the Sheep Meadow in Prospect Park at one of those dumb demonstrations. You were wearing a purple skirt and a tie-dyed undershirt and then we met Ruth and Paulie, and Paulie and I tried to get lost. We hid behind the water pump building and nobody even knew we were gone until everyone started leaving when they found out there wasn't really gonna be a free concert. The Jefferson Starship, I think it was."

"Airplane."

"What?" Tricia asked, the spoon lifted above her bowl.

"The Jefferson Airplane," Carrie said. She poured another cup of boiling water into the teapot and sloshed it around.

"Oh. Well, anyway, I had my bike then."

Carrie took a sip of the watery tea and studied Tricia. She had been a child of hope, born during the second and next-to-last year of Carrie's only marriage. A lifetime with Roy in a brownstone in Brooklyn had seemed The Right Thing at the time. But he was so silent, so serious, so solid; she longed for laughter, a little play in her life, and ended up looking elsewhere.

"That was a three-wheeler. We got it at the secondhand store on Ninth Street, down near the YMCA. You didn't get your two-wheeler until we moved upstate, when we were caretaking the Johnson place."

"Was that when we were with Richie?"

Carrie stared into her empty cup. Other children, she thought, keep track of their lives by what teacher they had in third grade, or when they took that vacation to Disneyland. Tricia told time by houses and her mother's men.

"Listen, I don't have to go to work today, so maybe we can make some sandwiches and go out to Lake Merritt. It's pretty now, and it would be good for both of us. What do you think?''

"So if we were at Johnson's, I was eight, right?"

"Eight, yes. Do you want to go?" Carrie had been unable to paint the day before. She had begun to admit that even when Hawkins's killer was found, Tricia would still have other charges to face. It was bound to be a mess that would reverberate for years. She reminded herself that upheaval could be looked upon as a kind of cleansing, brutal perhaps, but clearing the way for new growth. Oh bullshit, she thought, it's just goddamn painful.

Tricia slurped some milk and put her spoon down, staring at the tabletop. "Yeah, okay, only let's drive out to Point Reyes or something. I don't want to see anyone I know."

"That's too far. I can't take the car out there. If it dies, which it might, we'd really be stuck."

Tricia made swirls in the puddle of milk. "Why don't you get that thing fixed? Or just get a new car. It's a bummer."

Carrie put the teapot in the sink. "Can't afford to. Your graduation pictures cost fifty dollars, I owe the chiropractor about a hundred and fifty, and Morrisey just canned me. I'll figure something out, but I want to take the day, just you and me, and see if we can forget about everything for a few hours. Then I'll be able to handle it all better."

"Listen," Tricia began, "I don't really want to hear your problems now. I've got enough of my own. It's your own fault anyway. If you had a real husband or a real job, things would be different."

Carrie was tired of apologizing for who she was and thought that was all behind her with Tricia, but here they sat, facing off. The girl was old enough now to stop blaming her for not being Mrs. Cleaver in a white ruffled apron and high heels, baking tollhouse cookies and mixing the Kool-Aid.

"Shit," Tricia said, as Carrie's eyes filled with unwelcome tears.

"Let's not fight," Carrie said softly. "Why don't we go to the lake for an hour, hang out near the water, and feed the ducks?"

Tricia shoved her chair back and stood up, fixing her gaze on Carrie for a long cold second. "Shit," she said. She stalked out of the kitchen and slammed her balled fist into the bathroom door. A sound that was neither cry nor shout came from her, but she didn't pause. The door to her room banged shut.

Carrie hesitated to get up. If she offered comfort, she would be rejected. If she didn't, there would be an aching inside her, to take away her daughter's pain. She reminded herself that she was the adult. "You okay?" she called, trying not to shout. The noise of the radio blaring from Tricia's room was difficult to overcome. There was no reply. Carrie knocked once on the door. "Trish, are you all right?" she shouted as she turned the doorknob.

Tricia jumped off the bed, eyes glittering. "Don't ever come into my room without knocking," she warned, standing in the middle of the floor to claim her territory.

Carrie had no heart for this. "I knocked. You didn't hear me because the radio was so loud. I thought I heard you crying."

"Me cry? I haven't cried since we moved from Fox Hill and I had to give my rabbits away." Tricia's defense— attack, Carrie thought. She had heard the story four times a year since 1973, when she had said, no, they couldn't take the rabbits back to Brooklyn because they were going to stay with her friend Barbara, who had a three-room apartment and two children of her own. The accusation no longer had all of its original power to make her feel inadequate. The repetition had worn that down.

"Listen, I changed my mind. I don't think we should go anywhere, but maybe we can at least get through the rest of the morning without fighting."

"You mean we should be like normal people?" Tricia glared.

There was little chance for peace, but maybe another major battle could be averted. "I'm sorry about the rabbits," Carrie said. "I'm sorry about the car, and I'm sorry that you didn't hear me knock on the door. Let's stop fighting."

Tricia sat down on the edge of her bed, picked up a sneaker that was lying on the floor, and shook it. Two dimes and a penny rolled out. "Sure, Momma, sure." She stretched out her arm and let the sneaker drop with a thud. "Hey, you wanna go to the movies later, like a five o'clock show?"

Carrie, grateful for the truce, agreed. She closed the door without asking Tricia to turn the volume down. Now with the day before her, unfilled by work or plans, she felt uneasy. Okay, she thought, so I can't paint, but I can work in the yard. First she would dig up all the yellowing vines in the sad little plot that she nurtured and composted into an almost genuine garden, get rid of the winter peas. Winter— she still couldn't get used to thinking of that rainy, dismal period between December and March as winter.

Thin high light, glaring reflection of sun on snow. Stacks of firewood bearded in white. Windows glazed with ice that spun rainbows onto the polished floor.

She shuddered. Leaving New York had felt right at the time. Jeff assured her that they would do fine selling the leather goods that they produced in the shared storefront of the craft cooperative, but by the time they arrived in California, people were no longer buying handmade raw-hide hats and suede vests, and Jeff wasn't up to taking care of himself and living with a woman of thirty-four and a thirteen-year-old girl with pubic hair and a mind of her own. He spent weeks trying to convince Carrie that it was destiny, that someone in California was bound to recognize her talent as a painter. Scant comfort then, and another bubble in her simmering frustrations now. Gardening; dig in the dirt; stop thinking.

She opened the toolshed door and stepped into the narrow shed. Open bags of peat moss and potting soil lay on the floor, their odors like a forest after a deep rain. Clay pots teetered in a stack that was nearing its limits, and shovels and trowels and rakes hung on the wall. Carrie reached out to the right and felt for the hoe. It wasn't there. What's so goddamn hard about putting things back where they came from, she thought, as she recalled Tricia's brow furrowing in resentment when she finally agreed to turn over the small patch that had been set aside for radishes.

Carrie moved back into the daylight and once again thought about Jeff. Maybe California hadn't turned out to be the visionary place that he had described, but at least he had given her something by leaving. After a month, Carrie had realized that she and Tricia were indeed alone and that she had better take charge of their lives. For her own sake, she resolved not to depend on anyone again, not to let her sexual needs overwhelm her into forgetting that she must provide for herself and her child. No more casual relationships that one day become as necessary as food and air, no more passion that burns out and leaves essential emptiness. No more.

She found the hoe leaning against the garbage can and worked energetically, getting rid of the spent vines, raking the earth, making holes with the trowel, spilling the seeds, covering over the tiny black and larger green ones with soft dirt, directing a gentle stream of water at each mound. Patience; miracles still happen, every time something grows or gives fruit. Three o'clock arrived. Time had passed without miracles; but also without pain.

"I'm going to take my shower now. I'll let you know when I'm out so you can take one before we go," Carrie said to the closed door. A mumble acknowledged that she had been heard. Humming, she grabbed a clean towel from the closet and looked at her watch, wondering if there was enough time for a bath instead.

Pale body dips into steaming water. Particles of dirt, earthworm skins, bird droppings come loose from the bottom of my feet. Leaves turn black under my fingernails and float to the top of the water, then cling to my navel and my breasts.

The shower was hot and fast, and she scrubbed vigorously, watching the stream of water carry away the emblems of her work.

"I'm out," she shouted as she passed Tricia's room. She pulled on her jeans and a white T-shirt with a tie-dyed purple medallion in the center, slipped on the wide silver bracelets and then stepped into her leather sandals, noting that they would have to be replaced soon. The strap at the big toe was almost worn through, but it would certainly do for a night at the movies. She looked on her dresser and the night table for her hairbrush, didn't find it, tried the bathroom, and walked to the studio, still searching.

"It's twenty of. We should leave in about five minutes," Carrie called as she passed Tricia's room.

"Did you see my red square earrings, Momma?" Tricia yelled as she opened her door. They reached the hallway at the same time and stood facing each other.

"You know, the sixties were twenty years ago," Tricia said. "Tie-dyed is dead." She walked past Carrie, moving piles of papers and picking up glasses and bowls in search of her earrings. There was a crash and the clatter of objects rolling to the floor. Carrie held her breath.

"Oh shit, Momma. Where are some old rags?"

Carrie ran through the kitchen to the entrance to her studio. Tricia was picking up the fine-pointed brushes, trying to shake them while stepping around a spreading puddle of linseed oil on the floor.

"Should I use the painting rags to clean it?" she asked, not looking up.

Carrie's head began to throb. Each of those brushes had been acquired over ten years, at the sacrifice of the respectable furnishings that inhabit other people's lives. They were extensions of her brain, her eyes, her hands. And they were now filled with tiny pieces of glass. Totally unusable. It would take weeks to clean them.

"Don't bother. Just leave me alone for a while."

"Oh shit, I said I was sorry. I was just looking for my earrings."

"No, you didn't say you were sorry, and it wouldn't make any difference. They're all ruined. Why do you think your earrings would be in here? I never wear your stuff."

"Sure, you're too busy trying to hold on to something that's gone. And trying to suck me into it, too."

Carrie stooped to mop the spreading puddle. Small knots clumped in her shoulders and she pushed her elbows up and back to relieve the pain. "And you're so busy doing your own thing, being cool, that you don't see that there's more to life than square earrings. You're a self-centered child and you'll be a lonely self-centered adult."

"Take after my mother then, wouldn't I?" Tricia's voice was mocking, and Carrie didn't look at her.

"Just get out of here," Carrie said softly.

Tricia turned and ran down the hall. "Bitch!" she yelled, as the door banged shut.

Carrie picked up one of the brushes, smoothing the sable hairs along her palm. It felt soft, downy, and unprotected, and a thin sliver of glass gleamed as she fanned the hairs. She gathered all the others, rolled them in a sheet of newsprint, and knelt near the oil, dabbing at the edges with a painting rag that lay on the floor.

She used four more rags to wipe up the linseed and

started for the kitchen to throw them out. Tricia stomped into the living room just as Carrie reached the door.

"I'm getting out of here. I can't take this anymore." She was wearing the same gray jacket she had had on Sunday night, and the bright red sweater gave additional color to her face. A blue backpack dangled from one arm and she held her bicycle pump in the other hand. Carried worked to unlock her brain.

"Wait, Trish. We got upset, but it will be all right." I forgive you, she thought, they're only brushes.

"Yeah, well it's not all right with me." Tricia pulled the door open and ran down the stairs two at a time, not turning when Carrie called her name, not hearing Carrie say, "Oh, God, what now?"

# 16

"I don't believe it." Cruz smiled and looked at his watch. "I made it on time to Tuesday's soccer practice, and now it looks like I'm going to get there today, too."

"And I may even have time for a shower before dinner," Goldstein said. "I'm glad I have a date tonight; I could use some distraction after all those meetings. They weren't very pleased that I sat on Oneida without telling them."

"Don't lose sleep over it, man," Cruz said as he put two pencils in the groove of his top drawer. "They're gonna be heroes and they know they have you to thank for it." And maybe now I get back a full-time partner, not a cop with his mind a million miles away, he thought.

"I called Ronson a while ago," Goldstein said. "Intelligence has a watch on all the houses that we've identified and they got listening orders from the Feds. With a wire, the Hawkins thing is bound to come out."

"So you think I should drop the other stuff I've been working on, forget about the dog and all those people that Hawkins messed with?" Cruz shrugged into his jacket.

"No, don't forget about them," Goldstein said quickly. "Until we have more proof and it's all in our hands, keep at them." He walked to the door.

"Good night, man," Cruz said. "Have fun."

"I certainly plan—"

The phone rang. Goldstein started to say something, but Cruz interrupted.

"I'll get it. You go ahead. Probably Elenya reminding me about the soccer game."

The phone rang for the third time.

"Sure you don't mind?" Goldstein asked, but Cruz already had the receiver in his hand and was waving him out the door.

"Cruz, Homicide."

The voice on the other end was low, and the words sounded as if they were being forced out of the speaker's throat.

"I want to talk about Clifford Hawkins."

Cruz tried to identify the voice. It wasn't anyone on the force, unless they were new. Maybe it was another reporter. "Who is this?" He took out a yellow pad, preparing to write a name, information.

"It don't matter. You know who wasted him yet?"

Cruz turned the recording device to ON, all his senses alert. Calls like this were common during a well-publicized murder investigation. The callers were usually either pranksters or people with dull lives and active imaginations.

"Why don't you tell me who you are? We can talk better if that's clear."

"This'll have to do, sucker."

Male, hard to tell the age. Normal voice was being distorted. Maybe the lab could do something with the tape.

"Well, what do you want to tell me?" Cruz scribbled circles on the top sheet of the pad.

"I don't want to tell you, I want to ask you. Why haven't you busted Tricia Rayborn yet?"

"Look, if you have something to say, some information, then why don't you say it? I'm really busy, you know what I mean?" He had fifteen minutes to get to the playing field, plenty of time if he left right away.

"What would you think if I told you that Clifford

Hawkins grabbed her little titties, back in the alley behind the store?" The caller laughed, a quiet sound that was very different from the rasp of his disguised voice. "She pushed him off of her and grabbed an Orange Crush bottle and threw it at him."

"Why don't you come down to the precinct and sign a statement?" Cruz was uncomfortable. The voice was taunting, just beyond his ability to identify the speaker.

"Not me, sucker. You bastards will have to do it without me."

"Listen, man, I don't like being called names." This wasn't strictly true; it was part of life, after all, especially if you were Mexican-American and a policeman. He just wanted to keep the caller talking as long as he could.

"If you don't wanna know the rest, I'll hang up."

"If that's what you're gonna do, I can't stop you, can I?" Cruz wrote on the yellow pad. Harrison. Franklin. Hernandez. Marsten Rayborn. Oneida. All connected to Hawkins.

"She said she'd get him. Said he didn't deserve to live." The gruffness in the voice was less pronounced. Cruz listened harder; the voice was almost familiar.

"A lot of other people might have had the same feelings about Hawkins," Cruz said. Okay, draw him out. "He did hurt a lot of people, didn't he?" Tell me something. Give yourself away, man.

"He was evil, bad, and nasty. A *sadist* and a *thief*. Good thing someone did him in, right?"

"I'm not God, man. I just see that the law is carried out." Goldstein's the philosopher, not me, he thought.

"Yeah, well, whoever did it was right to blow him away. That thief isn't going to do nothing to no one else."

"Listen," Cruz said, "if you saw who did it, or if you have a gun, or know something that you're not telling me now, maybe we can meet and talk about it."

"Maybe I'll be in touch again." The words were spoken softly and then the line was dead.

Cruz listened to the tape four times, trying to catch a slip, a change in tone that was just out of his reach. Someone from the neighborhood, it would have to be, to have witnessed an encounter between Tricia and Hawkins in the alley. If the event had occurred at all. If it had, then there was a possible motive. Would Tricia Rayborn have killed Hawkins because he touched her breasts? Or had there been more to it? He would bring the tape to the sound lab, then confront Tricia with the story.

There goes soccer practice, he thought, as he dialed Elenya to tell her he would be late.

Her reaction will tell me what I need to know, Cruz thought, as he drove toward Fairfax Avenue. Now I have a wedge. A pink and orange sunset bounced off his side mirror as he parked near the grocery store. No, Tricia Rayborn, tough as she liked to think she was, wouldn't stand up to this kind of pressure . . . if the caller was telling the truth.

He rang the bell next to the Rayborn name. Had he really spent the past three days waiting for people to buzz him into their lives? He stepped back to look up at the studio windows. Carrie Rayborn looked down at him, then disappeared. The answering buzz was short and harsh.

# 17

Carrie stood with one hand on the worn finial of the stair railing, the other stuffed into the pocket of her sweater. It was Cruz; the height and the shape of his head, the square shoulders, and the solidity of his body were unmistakable. What did he want?

"Sorry. I don't answer until I know who it is. All the reporters, and even before that. It feels safer."

"Sure. That's smart," Cruz said. He too put his hands in his pockets. Carrie waited. It was his opening.

"Can I come inside? I want to talk to Tricia."

Carrie stepped into the apartment and Cruz followed, hands still in his pockets. Carrie felt the blood rushing around in her body, through passages that suddenly were too small.

"Tricia's out right now," she said. "I can have her call you when she gets back." Forced smile, bumping heart. "I thought it would be okay if she went out bicycle riding with some friends. You know, even in prison, they get some exercise, so I told her to go ahead. She just left."

"When will she be back?" Cruz asked. The kettle began to whistle and Carrie glanced at the clock above the stove, adding an hour to the time. He would certainly have better things to do than hang around here all that time, she thought. He'll leave and try again tomorrow. I'll find her by then.

"I'll wait," Cruz said. He smiled, a good guest.

"Tea?" Carrie asked.

"Sure," Cruz said.

Carrie pulled two unchipped cups from the drain and poured the splashing water into the brown ceramic pot, concentrating on keeping her voice light and her hands steady.

"What is it you want to talk to her about? Anything I can help you with?" Her eyes flitted from his face to the cups, back to his face.

"No, I really have to talk to Tricia." He stirred his tea with long, slow motions. Carrie wished he would look at her, give her some sign that he wasn't concealing terrible news behind his small movements.

"My child is in trouble and I have a right to know what's going on," she said. "It's too important to play games about."

The only sound in the room was the clink of the spoon as Cruz laid it in the saucer. He put his hands palms down on the table and broke the lock of their eyes.

"I know what you're saying," he said. "Believe me, I wish it could be different, but I have to do it this way."

Carrie looked past the alcove to the diminishing light of late afternoon and shivered; Tricia was out there somewhere. A spasm of pain grabbed at her lower back as she thought about the last time she sat waiting for her daughter to come home.

"Is there someone maybe that you could call, tell Tricia to come home so that I can talk to her?" Cruz shifted his legs. "It's getting late."

"No," Carrie said, looking into her cup. "I told you, she's out riding with some friends."

"You do know that home detention rules don't allow—" His words were interrupted by the ringing of the telephone.

Carrie jumped, afraid to answer; so much turmoil had come into her life over the phone during the past week. But she was more afraid not to answer it. It might be Tricia. I'll be home soon, Momma, she'd say. I'm sorry, Momma.

"Hello," Carrie said, moving with the phone as far into the studio as the cord would go. Cruz shouldn't hear their conversation.

"Good evening, Carrie. Jason here."

"Oh, hi, Jason," she answered, deflated. The gallery owner.

"I have absolutely marvelous news for you, so I won't put off for another second delivering what I'm sure will be the best thing you've heard all week, since that awful mess with your daughter started. How is she holding up, anyway?" Breathless, right to the point, as usual.

"We're all fine. What's the news, Jason? I've got a visitor and I don't want to leave him alone in the kitchen too long."

"You sly dear. Some new and elegant young man in your life and you didn't even tell Jason. And I thought I was your friend."

Carrie sighed. How could she possibly do business with a man who simpered so? She walked into the alcove and looked at Cruz's back as he sat at the table. He seemed like satisfying company compared to a protracted conversation with Jason Tremaine.

"Jason, why don't you just tell me why you called?"

"Oh, it's too absolutely delicious. You, my dear, are now four thousand dollars richer, and it doesn't seem to be over yet. Of course"—he giggled—"I'm delighted to be the instrument of this. Three separate people came into the gallery, yesterday and today, terribly eager to see your work. And between them, they walked out with two of the tiny acrylics and four of the *Opposite Shores* series. And they said they'd be back."

"Oh, Jason, that's really wonderful." Carrie sat down on

the floor and leaned against the wall. Her free arm hugged her own waist in congratulations. "The money . . . oh, God, it's really true. When you need something it comes to you." She thanked Marty, bless his encouraging universe.

"Well, dear, I have the check in my hand right now and will send it off posthaste." He was sharing her glee, as well as reveling in his own delight at receiving a commission. Maybe Jason, too, was really all right.

"That's terrific, Jason. What incredible timing. I needed a boost. A little well-placed recognition as a painter . . . better, even, than the money."

"My dear, people already know your name. In fact, those two gentlemen came in, they said, because they had seen you, or more accurately, heard you, on the telly. They said that all that wonderful publicity you were getting should make your paintings double or even triple in value, especially if there is a trial. What do you say to increasing the prices, ever so slightly, to say twice the current list?"

Carrie was silent. Too much. It was all too much. Too much greed and too much stupidity. Too much shock and too much terror. Too goddamn much.

"No," she said.

"But, my dear, now is the time to make the most of things, get ourselves known with the collectors. We have a virtual duty to capitalize on the scads of publicity. Why, your name recognition has risen dramatically this week, and the fickle public will forget it, if we let them. I have been trying to get hold of a friend, someone really good, sympatico and well-connected, to do an interview with you. We must make the most of what we are given." Paternal.

"No, Jason. No more sales until I say so. And no interviews. If you disregard what I'm saying, I'll pull out of your gallery."

"But, Carrie, my dear girl, my attorney has advised me that it is proper to do what I can to increase sales."

Carrie was calm. She noted, amazed, that her heart was

not banging in her chest and her breathing was regular and deep. "Jason, I've read that contract. There is a provision that permits me to withdraw from the gallery if you act unethically. So just don't show or sell any more of my paintings until you hear from me."

He mumbled a hasty good-bye and Carrie set the receiver in the cradle. All the years with only meager sales, all the gossipy art-world parties that she refused to attend because they were such a dishonest means of making a name, all the good paintings that languished in the galleries unsold while the darlings of the publicity mongers got rich and famous, played the game. And now the game was playing her.

> White queen, madonna in the center of the board.
> Black castles and bishop swarm around the white
> pawn. The queen wobbles and the pawn shrinks,
> smaller and paler. They melt in a milky puddle.

To benefit from Tricia's trouble was the ultimate irony in this senseless world. Yet she had no job and no money. The voice of cold logic demanded that she milk the goddamn sensation-hungry public, raise the prices of her work, and amass a lot of money. And now was the time to do it, hot irons and all that.

But she wouldn't and she knew it.

"Sorry that took so long," Carrie said to Cruz, who appeared not to have moved. "Business."

"Your boss?"

"No, my gallery," Carrie said. "I've just sold six paintings to people who don't know and don't care about the quality of my work, but think that the notoriety of Tricia's case is worth something. They expect the work to be worth even more, if she's charged with the murder." She stared at the table.

"Sounds like good news to me," he said. "You need money and now you got it, with the chance to make more."

"I don't want people to buy my paintings so that they can say, 'Look, I have something done by the mother of that girl who is on trial for murder.'" Carrie got up and took the teacups to the sink. She squeezed out a sponge and swiped at the table, cleaning imaginary crumbs.

"Where's Tricia, Mrs. Rayborn?" Cruz said, rising to stand beside her near the stove. "She's not really out riding, is she?"

# 18

All right, Goldstein thought, as he waited for the mirror to clear. Hawkins realized that Oneida was as repressive as public schools and minimum wage jobs for him and he wanted out. They cajoled and finally threatened, so he reverted to the behavior that had worked all his life to get him out of intolerable situations—mean, destructive acts inflicted on the nearest vulnerable objects, he hypothesized as he changed the blade in the razor, examined his face for blemishes, and lathered his fine stubble. Eventually he could count on being expelled. Only, this time the expulsion was permanent.

Oneida had no other option; Hawkins was beginning to call attention to himself and to the house. They had to kill him. That's especially plausible, he concluded as he held his nose up and drew the razor down to his upper lip, if they were about to conduct small-scale tests and were desperate to ensure the success of the planned coup.

So how does Tricia Rayborn fit into this fine theory, the car, the dog? Assume that her story is mostly true—the party, the joyride, picking up the Martinez girl, crashing. That would make Tricia's testimony convincing, he thought, wiping the last bit of shaving cream from under his chin. Okay, let's rearrange things. Tricia didn't do it, but she knows who did. Then one possibility, he thought, as he folded the towel over the bar and grabbed his white robe from the door hook, is that the other girl fired the shots. Still, the motive and the weapon are missing, he mused, stepping into his brown slacks and reaching for a white sweater. He bent to tie his shoes, pondering the problem of how best to verify this theory and then stood to examine himself in the full-length mirror. The doorbell rang, three quick, urgent blasts.

"Who is it?" He opened the peephole and met Tricia Rayborn's eye.

"Me. Tricia," she answered, looking back at him.

He opened the door, surprised at the materialization of his thoughts. Tricia walked into the middle of the room, picked up the smallest of the San Ildefonso vases from the mantel, and said, "Nice place. Furnished, huh?"

"If you mean, did it come that way, no. I chose it all myself. I like white."

"Yeah, and Indian pottery and modern art," she said, examining the standing water jar. "Well, aren't you going to ask me to sit down or something?"

"Sorry, I don't mean to be rude, but I have an appointment in ten minutes. What can I do for you, Tricia? Aren't you supposed to be at home? Where's your mother?"

Tricia deposited her backpack in the corner and stood in front of the white sofa, brushed off the seat of her jeans, and sat down. "My mother. She's home worrying about her precious paintbrushes. Could you give me a brandy? I feel a little shaky right now, and that would help." She crossed her legs at the knees and leaned forward, elbow on knee, chin on fist.

Goldstein frowned, annoyed that he would be late, and wary of a replay of the scene at the Rayborn flat. "Isn't this a little dramatic?"

"Dramatic, sure, it's dramatic all right, to be a murder suspect with your name all over the newspapers. Dramatic, that's it, to have a mother who cares more about her precious art supplies than she does about her own daughter." She drummed her fingers on her knee.

"Listen, I don't know what you mean, talking about art supplies and paintbrushes, but obviously something has happened to upset you." He tried to decipher what her eyes were saying. What was he going to do with this girl who was sending him all the wrong signals?

"I'm tired of it, her weirdness and her blaming me for things. She'd like it if that boring hippie scene was still happening. You're different. I can tell you care about me." She sprang up and stood in front of him. "And I really care about you."

For the second time, Goldstein felt the shock of her body being pressed against his, sensed the strain in her, and felt that she was not a child. She stood on her toes and whispered in his ear. "Please take care of me."

He pulled away from her, gathering his composure. It wasn't supposed to be this way; it should be Carrie, not her seventeen-year-old daughter. Actually, it should be Joan, who was probably writing him off at this moment.

"Tricia, you're confused. Things are hard for you now, and you're just barely handling it. Frankly, I don't blame you—everything's still unresolved, and it's difficult to live with that." He left her standing in front of the sofa and walked to the glass-topped table. "I'm going to call the woman I'm taking to dinner and tell her that I'll be an hour late, and then I'm going to drive you home. We can talk in the car."

"Never mind, I have my bike here. I'll see you later," she said, shrugging into her backpack.

"No, Tricia, I'm taking you home. We have some things that we have to get straight, just you and me, and I think it should be done now. We can lock your bicycle in the storage room downstairs, and I can bring it over another time."

Tricia's arms hung at her sides. "Yeah, sure," she said, "I don't know why I thought you were different."

The Oakland Bay Bridge was surprisingly free of traffic, and a gray, even mist blanketed the streets. Tricia had been quiet, looking out the window, never at him, but Goldstein twice pulled over to the curb and made her answer his questions, made her say yes, she understood why he had to avoid even a hint of personal involvement during the investigation of a case, and why, even if they had met under other circumstances, they moved in different worlds, had different interests, and would never have the sort of relationship she thought she wanted.

They parked half a block from her house, and by the time they reached the door, Tricia's hair, damp from fog and sweat, clung in patches to her neck and forehead. Carrie stood in the doorway and said "Trish" in the same tone, a mix of anxiety and relief, that he had heard when she first walked into the Juvenile room where Tricia and Angela sat, just three days ago.

"Where were you? I was so worried."

"Can I please go to my room? You're in my way," Tricia demanded.

"Cruz is here," Carrie said in a whisper, and then went pale as Goldstein stepped inside. "Oh God, what's going on? What are you both doing here?"

Tricia retreated quietly into the hall and started for the stairs. Goldstein gently moved Carrie aside in time to see Tricia bound past them onto the landing and take two steps at a time down the narrow flight.

"Trish, come back," Carrie shouted, gripping the handrail.

Four strides behind Tricia, Goldstein started toward the first landing. He knew he would be able to grab her once she reached the door. Suddenly, Tricia's left foot twisted and crumpled under her. Her eyes filled with tears, and her whole body shook.

"No, no, no, no, *no*," she shouted, trying to stand and falling back into a heap. "I have to get out of here." Her voice rose as Goldstein put his hands under her arms and lifted her to a standing position. She kept her left foot off the ground and talked to herself as he draped her arm over his shoulder. "I'm gonna get my bike and get out of here and no one will know where I am. I have to get out of here. Where's my pack?"

"Shhh," Goldstein said. He passed her a handkerchief, and she held it limply, still talking about her plan.

"No, let her be," Carrie said, stepping onto the landing. "This is the first time since Sunday that she's letting some of it out. She can't go around with all that fear and anger forever. Let her say it." She walked to the other side of Tricia, and put the girl's other arm around her shoulder.

Tricia's body shook with sobs, and Goldstein, uncomfortable, watched as Carrie reached up with her free hand and brushed the damp hair from Tricia's forehead. He looked up to the top of the stairs at Cruz and remembered that, two hours ago, his partner was preparing to leave for soccer practice. On time twice in one week, he'd said. Jay felt a bit of fear in his own heart, for Carrie and Tricia Rayborn.

"We're going to go real slow, Tricia," Carrie was saying. The girl took long, deliberate breaths, pushing back the remnant sobs. "Don't step on your left foot and we'll carry you up the stairs. I think your ankle's sprained."

They began the climb, Tricia subdued and yielding, Carrie and Goldstein lifting and stopping, gently bearing her weight. Cruz opened the door and cleared some magazines off the sofa, brought a chair from the kitchen, and set a pillow on it. Carrie secured an ice-filled towel to Tricia's ankle and then took her hand, not speaking. Goldstein motioned Cruz into the kitchen.

"What's going on?" he said, dabbing at his own forehead with a paper towel. "What about the soccer game?"

"I'll tell you in a minute. What are you doing with the girl, man? Her mother told me she was out riding her bike, but it didn't sound right to me."

"She was riding her bike. She rode it all the way through Oakland, over the bridge, and to my apartment in San Francisco. She had a fight with her mother, and came to me all confused about things. Now, what are you doing here?"

Cruz shook his head. "This is getting too personal, man. Watch out."

"I don't need lectures, Cruz. I'm standing here missing a date and I'm not even sure what's going on myself."

"All right, man, we'll talk about it another time. Remember that phone call, right when you were leaving? It turns out that somebody says Hawkins accosted Tricia in an alley, claims that he heard her say Hawkins didn't deserve to live."

Goldstein looked past Cruz into the alcove at Tricia and Carrie still sitting silent and immobile. "Who made the call?"

Cruz shook his head again. "He wouldn't say. Changed his voice. The more I listened to the tape of the call, the more it bothered me. There's something about the words, the voice . . . I don't know if I believe him, but this is the time to hit her with it. She's open now and I'm going in there and find out if there's anything to it."

Goldstein didn't stop him.

"Tricia," he said softly. Mother and daughter looked up, but Cruz spoke only to Tricia. "About four days before Clifford Hawkins was killed, he grabbed you in the alley near the grocery store and began to assault you sexually. You picked up a bottle and hit him with it, yelling that he didn't deserve to live. Isn't that right, Tricia?"

Goldstein stared at the girl. I have gotten too close, he thought to himself. What if she says yes?

"Yes," Tricia said, letting go of Carrie's hand and holding the ice tighter around her ankle. "That's right. He was an animal and I didn't want him to hurt me the way he hurt Charlie Hernandez and that little girl down the block. Yes, that happened." She winced in pain as she took the towel off her foot.

"Why didn't you tell me, Trish?" Carrie asked. "We could have done something about it."

"I think Tricia did do something about it." Cruz stood in front of them, hands in pockets.

"No," Tricia said, calm and dry-eyed. "If you mean I killed him, you're wrong. I tried to be his friend, but he was too twisted up inside to let me. I didn't kill him. I know you think I did and maybe it looks that way, but I didn't."

"But you drove the car while Angela did, isn't that right, Tricia?" Goldstein put up a wall between his mind and his feelings. The room was still; four breaths were drawn in and let out, each to its own rhythm. "Isn't that so, Tricia?"

"I must have been crazy to think you were a human being," Tricia said, color again rising in her cheeks. "And *you* must be crazy to think Angela killed anyone. She could never do anything to hurt anyone. You're both nuts."

Carrie bolted to her feet. "I think she's right. You are both nuts, and getting pretty desperate to badger her like this. Unless you can prove your charges, you'd better get out of here."

"Look," Cruz said, backing away toward the table, "we can't leave anything out. We have to check it all."

"Sure, but do you have to do it now, when she's hurt and confused and afraid? Would you like it if your children were treated this way?"

Goldstein stepped in front of Cruz. "When a murder happens," he said, "nothing is normal. We'll be in touch, tomorrow, the next day." He opened the door and waited while Cruz went into the kitchen and returned with his notepad. "Stay home, Tricia," he said, as he walked out the door, "and call us if you want to tell us anything."

They walked down the stairs and onto the street in silence. "We're blowing this one," he said to Cruz as they passed the darkened grocery store. "We're missing something."

# PART

# 6

# FRIDAY

# 19

"Hey, babe, shake yourself awake and listen good."

Goldstein rolled his head closer to the telephone, which lay beside him on the pillow. The clock said 5:30, and the angle of light as it fell on the ivory carpet confirmed that it was early morning.

"Mother?"

"Yeah, babe. Is your brain ready for big news? Don't matter. This will wake you up."

Goldstein sat up and pulled the electric blanket to his chin, eyes still closed. Mother sounded as though he hadn't slept all night. "Okay, all right. I'm ready," he said.

"That Oneida test run is today."

Goldstein's eyes opened and he reached for the notepad and ballpoint pen he kept on the bedside table. "You did good," he said, "as always. What's the plan and where will it happen?"

"I don't know how to tell you this. I don't know anything else. The kid got a message to me. Seems the little guys get fed their orders one step at a time. He doesn't know what or where either. Only that it's going down today. Orders are to be ready to move at seven-thirty this morning."

Goldstein settled back into the pillows. The Intelligence details that were posted at each of Oneida's houses would keep up with them.

"You still there, babe?"

"What else did he say? He still doesn't know anything about Hawkins?"

"Naw. Says they never even talk about the dude. Said he'd call back if he had the chance. That was all he told me."

"Okay. I'll be at my office in about an hour. If you hear anything else, call there."

Play it by the books, he thought, and call Intelligence, tell them what I just heard, keep them off my back about withholding information. He dialed the number and left word with Carrington about the Oneida action. If Mother could only come up with part of the story, he'd have to figure out the rest himself.

He sat on the bed, folded his legs in front of him, and took long breaths, counting to eight on the intake and to eight again as he let the air out. By the third breath, he felt his arms and shoulders relax, and on the fourth exhale he visualized all conscious thought being swept from his mind, leaving it white and floating and empty.

It took a while to achieve the first moment of real quiet, and it was disturbed immediately by the maps. First Khamir's, then MacPherson's, yellow lines, red circles, arrows. He pushed the images away and took four more deep breaths. Clarity, emptiness at last. He was bodiless, mindless, pure light and air, drifting. As though the meditation was a cloak he could put on at will, he felt himself covered, surrounded by a soft brilliance, and he listened to the paradox of knowing no consciousness.

Then, like a gnat worrying at his ear, the maps were back, and he unwillingly followed the images as they unfolded, trying to discover what his own mind was telling him. His ankles ached from the pressure, a sure sign that the meditative state had dissolved. He touched his forehead to the mattress and stood up slowly.

So close, he thought, and settled for reminding himself

that perfection was only an idea. He took a container of yogurt from the refrigerator, stirred the fruit from the bottom, and ate without thinking.

The third map! It was different. The pointer kept moving past the arrows, to the middle of the bay. Why? What was out there? Alcatraz, Angel Island, Treasure Island, the two red rockpiles jutting out of the water near the Richmond Bridge. The pointer, the pointer.

Angel Island. Former Civil War garrison, former immigration station, former Nike missile base. A state park now, served by two ferries. Marked trails, a sandwich shop. The place that all the arrows and the pointer led to. This was surely where the exercise was to take place.

Call Ronson first. Intelligence should stay out of his way long enough for him to somehow find out about Oneida's role in Hawkins's death. He dialed Ronson's number, waited while the phone rang four times.

"Hello," a sleepy female voice said.

"Hi, Mary, this is Jay Goldstein. Sorry if I woke you, but I have to talk to Mickey. It's important." He dumped the empty yogurt container in the garbage, rinsed the spoon, and paced.

"He's not here, Jay. He just left."

"If he calls, please make sure he picks up his messages at the station. As soon as he can."

"Sure," she said. "I will."

He hung up, dialed Ronson's number at headquarters.

"Intelligence, Carrington."

"Carrington, this is Goldstein again. I need to talk to Ronson. It's urgent."

"Sorry, Goldstein, he's not here. Can I do something for you?"

"Damn," Goldstein muttered.

"Sorry, I didn't get what you said," Carrington said.

"Look, get this message to Ronson or someone else who is working on the Oneida thing. They're planning some kind of action today on Angel Island. I don't want those guys hanging too close. Khamir is jumpy, and he might spot a tail if they're not careful. And that would blow it for my case. Tell them to keep their distance." They could all get what they wanted, if they were smart.

"You planning to go to Angel Island?" Carrington asked.

"Look, I don't have time to chat, Carrington. Just deliver the message."

"Okay, Goldstein, but don't do anything dumb. Your pinstripes might give you away."

"I have other calls to make, Carrington. Thanks for the advice." He hung up and dialed Cruz's house.

"Hello." Second sleepy female voice of the morning. That's how it is to be married to a cop, he thought.

"Sorry if I woke you, Elenya. Can I speak to Carlos?"

"That's all right, Jay. I wasn't sleeping. Carlos left real early, but I don't know where he went. You know how he is about telling me anything about work."

"Sure. Thanks anyway. I'll get him on the beeper," Goldstein said, annoyed that Cruz was gone. Where would he go so early, anyway?

"I don't think so," Elenya said.

"What do you mean?" Goldstein asked, alarmed. The captain had gone up one side of Delvecchio and down the other, not four weeks ago, for not having his beeper with him on a stakeout. The memo that had followed was crystal clear: gun, badge, and beeper, to be within reach at all times.

"It's here on the desk," Elenya said softly. "The batteries ran down, and he said he would get some last night, but I guess he forgot."

"Great, that's really terrific," Goldstein said. "Look, if you talk to him, tell him to call the office. I'll leave a message there."

*   *   *

"Okay, sure," Elenya said. "Hey, you going to the picnic next week?"

"What picnic?" he asked, looking through his bottom drawer for his oldest pair of jeans. "I don't know anything about a picnic."

"The one on Angel Island. Didn't Carlos tell you?"

"No," Goldstein said, his brain whirling, "he didn't say anything about it."

"The soccer team. It's an annual thing, and he wanted you to come."

His laugh released the fear that had bubbled up at the mention of Angel Island. "We'll see. Take care, Elenya."

He looked at the clock. He would make the first ferry, and hope that he could track Khamir and the rest before they spotted him. He called Homicide, left word for Cruz that he was going to Angel Island, and dressed.

Goldstein looked at himself in the mirror. Jeans and a blue cotton shirt, yellow sweater tied over his shoulders. He slipped his small tape recorder and the Minolta into his camera case. The very picture of a man with a day off, eager for sun and solitude. He took off the yellow sweater, replaced it with a worn black sweatshirt, and jammed a green and yellow A's cap down on his head. They would put Oneida out of business today, get Hawkins's killer. It's almost over, he thought. It will be tricky, especially without Cruz and no direct communication with Ronson. This morning, however, the universe seemed to be pointing him toward Angel Island, and he trusted that.

# 20

The thin blue curtain lifted slightly in the morning breeze and Carrie stopped to watch the feathery carrot greens dance and bend in the garden below. She hummed as she scooped up a pile of socks and shirts from the foot of the bed and dumped them into the wicker basket, then went to the bathroom, whistling as she turned on the hot water for her shower.

Dry and dressed, Carrie realized she was hungry. She wanted plates heaped with eggs and slices of salty bacon, English muffins with their nooks and crannies swimming in butter, pots of marmalade, tea with sugar and cream. She would take Tricia a tray and check the swelling on her ankle. One hand on the refrigerator, she stopped whistling. Tricia was in the living room, talking to someone whose voice Carrie didn't recognize. Adult male, not Marty or Goldstein or Cruz.

Her first impulse was to run into the other room, but she checked it and listened. Maybe she should go in there with a kitchen knife behind her back, or call for help. But Tricia was laughing and the male voice was soft. The knife and a muffin, one in each hand, a casual entrance, she decided, and ambled into the alcove.

"Who's here, Tricia?" she asked.

"A friend of Sergeant Goldstein's. Momma, meet Mother."

Carrie's eyes widened at the sight of the man standing in the doorway. He was at least six feet three, thin, very black, and grinning. She gripped the handle of the cleaver tightly.

"Good morning, Mrs. Rayborn. Making breakfast?" he asked. His voice was deep, rich, and the smile unnerved her.

"Who are you and what do you want?" She looked from Tricia to Mother. This better be good, she thought, and then you better get out of here.

"As your daughter said, I'm a friend of Goldstein's. An associate, to be more precise. I have to get in touch with him." He took his hands out of his pockets and leaned against the table.

"Why did you come here? Why don't you just go to the police station if you need to talk to him?"

"Now, Mrs. Rayborn, I wouldn't be bothering you if I could do something as simple as go to the police station. He's not there, he's not in his apartment, and his partner wasn't home, so I thought I might find him here." He lifted his hands in front of him, palms toward her. "Don't you think that cleaver is a bit much for cutting muffins?"

Carrie looked down at the knife and the muffin. She still didn't trust this man. Whatever he had said only added to her wariness.

"Sergeant Goldstein isn't here and I haven't the slightest idea where he might be. I think you'd better leave now." Maybe he's a goddamn reporter. Out, she thought, I want him out of my house now. "If you don't get out of here, I have no qualms about calling the police." She moved closer to the table. The phone was under a pile of papers, and she reached for it, muffin still in her hand. He just stood there, smiling and inscrutable. Goddamn.

"I have to get some information to him that will help him clear up the Hawkins murder."

Carrie started to waver. Until that was settled, everything in her life was on hold. The telephone rang. Carrie was too startled to move and Tricia reached for the receiver before Carrie could say anything.

"Hello," the girl said, her eyes on the floor.

"Who is it?" Carrie demanded.

"Shh, I can't hear him," Tricia said, covering the mouthpiece. She nodded once, then put her hand over the phone again. "You won't believe this. It's for him." She handed the phone to Mother.

Carrie watched in silence as the man nonchalantly held out his hand to accept the phone. He said little, smiled mysteriously, and then stopped. His left eyebrow arched high, lengthening his already drawn face, and he turned his back on Carrie and Tricia.

"Tell me again. Did he say what he was going to do about it?" Another nod, this time merely a bend of his head downward. Mother rummaged on the table, came up with a pencil stub, and starting writing on the corner of a newspaper clipping that had been lying on the table. "Okay, got it. I'm gonna get my ass down there, babe. You try to keep things cool until I get there." Silence. Rapid head-shaking. "Yeah, that's good. Be careful."

He hung up and Carrie waited, transfixed, oblivious to the knife and the muffin in her hand. Tricia broke the silence.

"Hey, what was that about?"

"An acquaintance just located Sergeant Goldstein." He tore off the top corner of the newspaper clipping and put it in his pocket. "Listen carefully, ladies. Our friend is in trouble. That boarding house across the street is a front for some lunatic terrorist organization."

"Terrorists?" Carrie repeated. Teheran, Belfast, Entebbe have terrorists. Not Oakland. Not lately.

"I don't have time for the details. They're dangerous and they just spotted Goldstein waiting for the ferry to Angel

Island. They know he's following them. I'm gonna get the next ferry, which won't be easy, seeing as it's the tail end of rush hour. You call Cruz. If he's not there, leave a message so that he's sure to call back. Tell him what's going on."

"Wait a minute," Carrie said, unbelieving. "Goldstein is in trouble, somewhere on a ferry boat to Angel Island?" Mother nodded and walked to the door. "Tricia will make the call. I'm coming with you. You'll be less conspicuous with a woman."

"Lady, there's nothing that will make me inconspicuous." He laughed. "And certainly not walking around with you." As he started out the door, Carrie grabbed his sleeve and he turned with a rush of air between his teeth. "I have to get out of here."

"I'm coming with you," she said quietly.

"What's going on? Why is the traffic so slow?" Carrie asked, impatient with the crawl of the cars inching along the MacArthur Freeway. "We can't miss the ferry."

Mother shot her an exasperated look. "It's all these people who think it's all right to pollute the air so that they can take their nice little weekend trips after work on Friday." He gripped the steering wheel tighter and flipped to the radio news station.

"Our Sky Guy tells us there is a thirty-minute delay at the toll plaza of the Bay Bridge. And an accident on Five-Eighty just east of—"

"Terrific," Mother said, snapping the radio off.

"There's got to be a better way. We'd get there faster if we walked," Carrie said.

Mother suddenly swung the car into the far right lane, veering close to a pickup truck and cutting in front of a white Mercedes with a startled blonde in the driver's seat.

"You're brilliant," he shouted, accelerating as he shot past another lane of traffic and headed for the Berkeley exit. "There is another way to get there. We're going the way the rich folks go . . . Marin County, here we come." He whooped and the speedometer showed seventy.

Carrie gripped the armrest as they rocketed toward Ashby, toward University, toward what felt like an imminent collision.

"There's another ferry," Mother said, grinning. "From Tiburon, where folks pay for their caviar at the local supermarket with American Express cards." They zipped past one more exit and headed onto a ramp. "We'll get there faster this way."

"If we don't die first," Carrie said, settling back and almost enjoying the blur of cars as they sped along. "Do you really think Goldstein is in danger?" His face crept into her brain, the blue eyes that always said more than his words, his lean hardness.

"I ain't in this car doing seventy-five because I want to bring him a birthday present," he said. "Yeah, he's in danger."

Bursts of flame outline the hills. He fires, I adjust my gun and lean over to check his arm. Blood, garnet-colored, seeps through his shirt. I touch my stained fingers to my mouth.

"Watch out, baby, here we come," Mother shouted as he passed a truck where the freeway ended and street began. "We got work to do."

# 21

Poor old lady, Cruz thought, as he stood on the front porch waiting for the shuffle and bump of Mrs. Franklin and her cane. I'm not gonna be the one to tell her. It will break her heart. Her daughter or the boy can have that job. He looked through the lace window curtain, but nothing moved.

Mrs. Franklin would know the dog in Carrie Rayborn's photograph. It had been at her house Sunday night. Unless I'm wrong, Cruz thought.

He walked to the back of the house, stepping carefully around the fuschias and hydrangeas that bordered the walk. The yard was small and well-kept, with a round redwood table and two chairs at one end and a clothesline with a worn bag bulging with clothespins at the other. He looked into the kitchen window. The counters were clear, the table empty, except for a lace cloth. He leaned over and saw four green potted plants in the sink. They all look healthy enough, he thought. Why would she put them in the sink?

He continued around the house, peering into all the windows. No sign of Mrs. Franklin. Old ladies, he thought, have been known to slip and fall. I don't want to find her dying or dead, clutching for the shower curtain. Slow down, man, he warned himself. Don't get carried away. You're a homicide detective. The bodies get easier, except for the children, and you've learned to see them as evidence. He stood on an old peach crate that was lying near the side of the house and checked the bathroom window. No body in the bathtub. He took a deep breath of relief.

He pushed back a low-hanging branch of a large persimmon tree that was heavy with hard green fruit and returned to the front of the house. The woman next door—Mrs. Franklin had said she was a nurse, a friend. Maybe she would know where the old lady was.

He approached the house on the left first. Two planter boxes on either side of the white door. A bright red welcome mat. Someday, Cruz thought, we'll live in a place like this, get out of that thin-walled apartment, give Elenya a study, let the boys each have a bedroom. They would cut the grass together on weekends, have the guys over for barbecues. Someday, he vowed, my yard will be full of roses and lilacs—the nicest on the block—although what block and what year, he didn't know.

"Hey, what are you doing there?" A woman stood on the sidewalk, blue coat open to reveal a white pantsuit uniform. The nurse. Cruz walked out to meet her.

"Hello. I'm Sergeant Cruz. I'm looking for Mrs. Franklin, but she's not home." He brought his shield out of his pocket and she looked at it carefully.

"Oh dear, is there any problem?" she asked. She was pretty; her blond hair was long, held back by a blue ribbon, and her mouth and eyes were at ease with the world, despite her obvious concern for her neighbor and her fatigue. Just coming off shift, he assumed.

"I have a couple of questions to ask her, that's all," he said.

"Poor thing, she broke her arm yesterday and her grandson Royal came and took her to the hospital. He called me to say that she was going to stay there with them, at her daughter's house, until she was doing a little better."

"Royal?" he said. "Do you have the address?"

"Oh, sure. It's inside." She started up the front steps,

pulled a sheaf of mail from the red box beside the door, and took out her key. "I'll be right out."

He waited on the porch while she disappeared into the house. The flowers in the planter were healthy; lots of sturdy bright green foliage and clusters of curly petals in the center. He'd have to start asking the names of things he liked, so that when it was time, he would know what to ask for.

The woman propped the screen door open with her right foot and handed him a slip of paper. He read the address, folded it, and put it in his pocket.

"Thanks. Sorry to bother you," he said, and turned to walk away. The screen door closed, then the heavy wooden door was pulled shut. Shit, he thought, I forgot to ask her about the flowers.

The house was more than a mile away. Maybe no one will be home, he thought. Maybe this won't be it. His pounding heart and sweating hands were sure signs, though. He couldn't remember when he had resolved a case without these signals; some part of him just knew when it was going to go down. He needed the weapon, the rifle from which the shot that killed Clifford Hawkins was fired. And he was about to get it. But it wouldn't be simple, almost never was.

The street looked a lot like Fairfax Avenue, full of middle-aged houses, never luxurious, now as well cared for as the scramble for money and time would allow. Everyone worked hard, but it was like fighting the incoming tide with a child's bucket. Sooner or later, Cruz thought, they would either be overwhelmed or the tide would recede and they would breathe easier. Things would appear to be safe, but the inevitable return of the high water would always take them by surprise.

One-sixty-seven Midvale. The name on the mailbox. Kerner. Why me? he thought, as he knocked on the door.

"Turn that down, Royal," a woman's voice called. "I

think there's somebody at the door. And put the dog in the bathroom." Light footsteps, a woman in bare feet sounded down the hall, and he knocked again.

"Who's there?" the voice asked.

"Sergeant Cruz, Oakland Police Department." He wiped his hands on the side of his pants.

"Yes?" she said as she opened the door. She was small and light-skinned, her hair in soft curls around her head. Her eyes were very dark and there was both a sharpness and a sweetness in her face at the same time. He wondered which he would get now.

"May I come in, Mrs. Kerner? I spoke to your mother earlier this week, and I just have a few more questions to ask her. I heard that she's had an accident, so I'll try not to take too much of her time." He waited for her to reply, but she was frowning. He took out his shield; her face relaxed a little.

"You understand—I can't just let anybody in who says he's a policeman."

Cruz told her that he understood.

"My mother is still pretty weak," the woman went on, "and the doctor said she needs her rest. She's healthy for a woman of eighty-six, but it's still taken a lot out of her." She led him to the front room, where Mrs. Franklin was reclining on the sofa, her right arm propped on three pillows.

"Morning, Mrs. Franklin. Sorry to hear about your accident," Cruz said.

"We old folks don't mind a bit of discomfort." Mrs. Franklin's voice was barely audible. "It's a reminder that we're still alive, don't you know." She offered a wink, and her breathing became labored from the exertion of her joke.

"This won't take long," Cruz said, as a door slammed somewhere in the back of the house, startling the old lady. Two voices shouted words that he couldn't make out, and a dog began yapping. Mrs. Kerner looked in the direction of the noise, disturbed.

"I'm more likely than ever," the old lady said, "to fall asleep on you now. Pain pills, don't you know." She reached her good hand up to her throat and adjusted the little white collar of her dress. All of her movements were slow; even the blinking of her eyes seemed to take longer than usual. The drugs, no doubt. There was a sudden flurry of shouts and another door slammed.

"Excuse me. I'm going to get those kids to settle down." Mrs. Kerner bustled out of the living room, leaving Cruz and the old lady alone.

"Better ask me what you want to know, Sergeant. Before I forget it."

"Have you ever seen this dog?" he asked, passing the photo to her.

She chuckled. "Can't see nothing without my glasses. Can't even read a label or see to knit without them for the past thirty years. Can't tell you until I put them on."

Cruz looked on the table tops and on the mantel. No glasses. He walked toward a short-legged curio cabinet near the doorway as a rush of footsteps, fast and strong, flew down the stairs, followed by the patter of a dog and the barefoot slap of Mrs. Franklin's daughter.

"Royal, what's got into you? Come back here!" The woman's voice was angry, and Cruz dashed into the hall as she reached the bottom step. He charged past her, following the boy toward the rear of the house.

"Royal, you stop now and come back here this minute!" she shouted behind him.

The back door banged shut, and Cruz pushed it open again. Royal, in a green and blue striped shirt and faded denims, was almost at the far boundary of the yard. He put both hands on the wooden fence and deftly tossed his body over. A white dog lifted its front paws to the fence and whined, wagging its tail, tried to jump, and fell back onto the grass, agitated. Cruz stopped at the fence just long enough to see the two patches of black around its eyes as the poodle stood crying for its companion. Then Cruz jumped over the fence too.

Shit, he thought, looking around the empty, weed-filled yard. I can't catch a nineteen-year-old boy on foot. He ran out to the sidewalk, stumbling over a broken yellow toy dump truck that lay on its back next to the house. Gone. I've lost him. One step farther away from closing this one. One step farther away from promotion and my house.

He vaulted the fence again, back into the Kerner yard. Mrs. Kerner was sitting on the back step, dazed, biting her lower lip. Her hands were jammed into her skirt pocket and she looked as though an earthquake rumbling through the yard wouldn't have moved her.

"Please, Mrs. Kerner. I don't have time to explain. Did your husband have a gun?" He watched her face intently.

"Yes, a hunting rifle. He used to go up to the Sierras every fall. What's going on?" She looked away from the spot where her son had jumped over the fence and vanished.

"It's very complicated. I have to find Royal. Do you have any idea where he might go? A friend's house? A favorite hangout?"

She stared at him, unmoving. "What do you want with him?" There were no tears; her eyes turned blacker, and she watched the fence.

This is it, Cruz thought. "He may have shot Clifford Hawkins."

She laughed, a shrill peal of notes filling the yard. "You're crazy. Royal is such a sweet child, always taking care of his grandmother. Straight-A student in college. You are crazy," she repeated.

"Mrs. Kerner, would you show me where you keep your husband's rifle? And then I want to talk to your other children."

The woman shook her head, still smiling, and opened the door to the garage.

"No, don't touch it," Cruz said as she was about to take the rifle down from a rack on the wall. He took his handkerchief from his pocket and gently removed it from the hooks. "Good, now please get the other children."

"You're wasting your time," she said. "Royal had a fight this morning with Thomas and he ran away to let himself cool down a little. Always does that when he's really angry. Which isn't very often. He'll be back in a while, hour or two, when he's all calm again." She shook her head as she walked up the stairs.

Cruz looked into the living room at Mrs. Franklin, who had fallen asleep with her mouth open and was snoring loudly. He heard voices, footsteps, and turned to see a boy, younger and stockier than Royal, standing beside a slender girl of about sixteen. Mrs. Kerner stood behind them, no longer smiling.

"I'm a police officer, and I want to find your brother. He may be in trouble, and he's only going to make things worse for himself by running away now. Do you know where he might be?"

They stood there, the boy, the girl, and the mother, expressionless and silent.

"Don't know where he went," the boy said finally, shrugging his shoulders.

"Yeah, he just went out," the girl added, as though jumping over the fence with their mother shouting after him to come back was the way Royal left the house every day.

Cruz knew he wasn't going to get very far, and half admired their solidarity. But he needed the boy. The gun would be proof—Ballistics would run their tests, send a report saying that the rifle's nicks and grooves matched the ones in the bullet. He had to find Royal. Sooner rather than later, for the boy's sake.

"All right, listen carefully. You'll be doing Royal a favor

if you help me find him. Or you can find him yourselves and give me a call. Resisting arrest is a serious charge." He looked into their frightened, confused faces. There are no easy answers, he wanted to tell them, and thought of Elenya and Julio being confronted with this dilemma. They would do the same, he thought.

He broke eye contact with the girl last, then picked up the rifle again with his handkerchief. He turned and walked slowly toward the door, listening for words or footsteps as he got farther away from the hall.

"Wait," the girl said, "I just thought of something."

Cruz stopped, holding his breath.

The girl's voice quavered as she spoke. "When he's angry or scared, he runs away. He gets on the bus and goes to San Francisco. Golden Gate Park."

"He's done this before?" Cruz asked softly, watching Mrs. Kerner, who put her hands on her younger son's shoulders.

"Yeah," the girl said. "Mom got real mad once because Royal forgot to mow the lawn. He didn't come home until supper time."

"And he went to Golden Gate Park?" Cruz asked.

"Yes," the girl said steadily. "I bet that's where he is now."

"You traitor!" the boy screamed, his fists balled tight. His foot shot out, hit the girl in the shin, and he broke away from his mother's startled hold and ran up the stairs. "Now they're gonna get him!" he yelled as he slammed a door behind him.

The girl bent down to rub her shin, tears of pain filling her eyes. "He's real attached to Royal," she said. "I want to get this over with, like you said. I think that would be better."

"You know," Cruz said, "if you aren't telling me the truth you would be obstructing justice. That's against the law."

Her eyes met his. "I know what's right and what's wrong," she said, "and I'm doing what's right."

"Mrs. Kerner, I'm going to take this rifle with me. And I'll call the San Francisco police to get some help finding Royal. If you have anything more to tell me, call me at this number."

He handed her a card and let himself out without looking back at them, two women standing in the hall. The girl is lying, he thought, and he pulled the door closed behind him. The white poodle with two black eye patches followed him all the way to the sidewalk, wagging its tail and sniffling at his shoes.

# 22

The bay was glassy and the sun leaped in the wake of the slow-moving ferryboat. Thick fog, white and fluffy, began to slink out through the passage below the Golden Gate Bridge, and for a moment Jay Goldstein was peaceful, rocking with the insistent forward motion of the craft. Five more minutes and they would land, or so he judged from the shrinking size of the city. He was sitting in a sheltered spot on the upper deck in the rear, as far from the group he was following as possible. Plenty of time for close contact when they got to Angel Island. They weren't going anywhere until then.

He watched the foamy wake, and pulled the cap down lower over his eyes when an unfamiliar figure, a roundfaced young man in the ubiquitious sweater and corduroy pants, walked by for the third time. Not someone from the Fairfax Avenue house, maybe not even someone from Oneida. He was standing against the railing looking out toward the city. Maybe he's just a tourist, Goldstein thought, checking out the landmarks. The man pushed away from the railing and started walking toward the narrow staircase that led to the lower deck.

As he passed, a folded piece of paper drifted from his hand onto the deck. Goldstein waited until the man was inside, and moved toward the paper. It skittered on the

170

deck; Goldstein knelt to pick it up. As he bent down, the boat lurched and bumped. He lost his balance and fell to his knees. The ferry must have docked, he thought, as a second soft jolt followed the first. The paper went over the side and floated toward the water.

No time to worry about it now, he thought regretfully, and certainly no way to retrieve it. Perhaps it was just a coincidence anyway. He ran to the stairs and reached the lower deck as the first passengers were stepping onto the ramp. The ferry had been full: teenaged boys and girls cutting school, Ronson and Makros in jeans and light jackets, a family of twenty noisy, laughing, dark-eyed Chicanos, babies and grandparents and young couples, and four men in suits, two with dark glasses. Now that J. Edgar was gone, you'd think they'd know better, Goldstein mused. And Oneida, thirty of them, as far as he could tell. From his place at the end of the line, Goldstein could make out Khamir's compact body up near the front; MacPherson's red hair and broad shoulders were part of a group stuck in the middle. He kept them in his sight as he walked up the freshly painted ramp. The crowd wound around through the mazelike fence that kept arriving visitors queued neatly.

On a hill to his right, an expanse of emerald lawn was dotted with picnic tables and stone barbecues. Below the lawn, on the other side of an asphalt path, was a small stretch of beach, empty of bathers, waves licking quietly at the sand. A sailboat bobbed prettily about fifty yards from the beach. Nice place, he thought, some other time.

The line of passengers had come to the end of the debarkation area and were beginning to disperse. Goldstein kept his eyes on the two familiar figures, and then began to pick out others—Soong and Sanchez were talking in front of the bathrooms just ahead, and the man who had dropped the paper on the rear deck was standing nearby. They were all there, in fact, standing close to each other. That's nice, he thought, makes it easier to keep track.

The thirty men clustered together and then, to Goldstein's consternation, split up into three groups. Khamir and several others headed in the direction of the snack bar, a second group hung back at the information station, and the rest, including MacPherson, made a left turn at the main road that circled the island. Ronson was sticking with the bunch at the information station and a pair of federal agents hung back near the other two groups.

For Goldstein to follow Khamir would be too risky. At least five people in that group might recognize him. Better to keep with MacPherson's entourage. The man's height and red hair made him easy to follow, and he had only seen Goldstein once.

Regretting that he couldn't split himself into three, id with Khamir, ego with MacPherson, superego with the third group, he walked slowly. The path MacPherson chose led to a steep climb up wooden steps with a rough-hewn handrailing on one side. The steps twisted up the hill to a height of one hundred feet in less than a quarter of a mile, but Goldstein felt strong, prepared by the daily workouts that increased his stamina and his lung capacity. He climbed effortlessly, taking long strides, and kept the green sweater of the last man in his line of vision. At the top of the steps, they stopped.

Goldstein bent down, his back to the group, and untied, then retied his shoelaces, waiting for sounds of movement. He thought about a high school composition assignment: write a ten-sentence paragraph explaining how to tie a bow. It had made him aware that there were parts of him that functioned without conscious effort, and became the kernel of his search to learn more about the nature of learning and the nature of being. Full circle, he thought, everything comes full circle. Shoelaces.

He turned his head slightly. MacPherson was pointing to the left, and one of the group walked off in that direction. Goldstein untied and retied his other shoe. Low voices, then footsteps. They were headed north.

He kept his hat pulled down and slumped his shoulders, watching as they went around a curve, then clambered up the final thirty feet to the broad macadam road. From this vantage, he could see the town of Tiburon directly across the water and, off to the right, the strange curves of the Richmond Bridge and the oil refineries beyond, a maze of stolid holding tanks and spidery pipes that belched fire in a thin stream. The Oneida group was proceeding at a steady pace around the island, and he kept his distance. When two of the men lagged behind and turned, cameras pointed in his direction, he stopped to examine a eucalyptus tree, concentrating on the delicate peeling bark and the powerful camphory smell of the leaves, letting go of tension as he focused all of his senses on the tree. The exercise left him sharper, calmer.

A father and son on bicycles whizzed by, and Goldstein increased his pace to regain the group. Even at this distance, they looked like an advance cadre: MacPherson up front, tall and imposing; a cluster of eight men, double file; and the rear guard. No casual collection, out for a stroll. But why Angel Island?

He had been here often, on family outings, his mother in stockings and walking shoes carrying a wicker basket that the housekeeper had prepared, filled with tiny sour pickles, pâté, Brie, bread, oranges. It was wonderful; he remembered thinking that he could see the entire world from here—his home on the southeast flanks of Mt. Tamalpais, the gleaming white city of San Francisco, its streets rising to the tops of hills like parts in the hair of a young girl, the faraway buildings of Berkeley and Oakland, the three bridges. The memory stopped him in his tracks.

Of course. You *could* see everything from here. All of the Bay Area. A perfect command post from which to control military actions in the towns and cities.

Goldstein was approaching a cluster of buildings, an old Civil War garrison of large, yellowing stone structures with

brass nameplates green with age in front of each building.
When he looked down the path, he was surprised to see only
eight of the original group he had been following still in
front of him. MacPherson and the rear guard were nowhere
in sight. He didn't like not knowing where they were.

He stepped off the path into a small patch of rhododen-
dron. This side of the island was usually isolated. He would
have felt better with the camouflage of a crowd, but this
would have to do. The group of eight was standing in a
bunch, near the entrance to one of the larger buildings, the
infirmary, he thought, as he scanned the area for signs of the
missing three. He listened and heard the water lapping at the
rocks below, then footsteps behind him.

He spun around to face one of the rear guard, the taller
one, a thin, lank-haired boy of no more than twenty, with
pale skin and light brown hair that was parted in the middle.

" 'Scuse me—do you know where a bathroom is?" the
boy asked.

Goldstein removed his hands from his pockets, ready to
use them if he had to. "Sorry." Goldstein shook his head.
He watched the eight men, still gathered at the same spot.
The boy smiled, his deep-set eyes scanning Goldstein's
face. Jay nodded, turned, and walked back to the path,
away from the group.

His ears were tuned to the sounds behind him, but there
was nothing. He went on to a bench twenty feet down the
path, and sat looking casually back to the spot where he had
stood a few minutes before. The group was gone.

He had to find them. A large truck with four park workers
riding atop a pile of tree trimmings rumbled by. There was a
big empty field ahead, and to the left a path strewn with last
season's fallen leaves. At the end of the path stood the
largest of the East Garrison buildings. All of its windows
were empty voids, and rusted fire escapes crisscrossed the
side of the building.

He took off his sweatshirt and hat, rolled them together,

and placed them under the bench. If there was a lookout, he would be watching for someone in a black sweatshirt. He listened. A woodpecker, slow and lazy in the inceasing heat of the morning. Wind in the eucalyptus. And voices. Male voices, somewhere ahead. There they were, going up the steps, into the big building at the end of the path.

Goldstein decided to approach from east of the building, where the dense undergrowth had not yet been cleared by the park crews. One of the branch-filled trucks came by, moving slowly with its precarious load, and he used it as a shield between himself and the building. Crouching low, he dove into the bushes, vaguely aware that the shiny leaves beside him were poison oak. Small price, he thought, allowing himself a brief projection of Carrie Rayborn's face when she learned that the murder charges wouldn't be filed against Tricia.

The wind changed direction and he smelled tar and seawater. All of his senses sharp, he was in that state of heightened acuity that made him feel that he was a conduit for some universal power. He heard voices.

First one voice, then a chorus followed, like the meeting he had seen from the porch of the Fairfax Avenue house. He crept a little farther; the bushes began to thin considerably, and he stopped. He took the camera case from his shoulder, extracted the tape recorder, and turned it on.

"And I will be strong, to help my country rebuild from the ruins of decadence," the voices intoned.

"And I pledge to maintain the secret of Oneida until it is proclaimed across the land by the liberated," the single voice said. It was MacPherson. He doesn't look like the hysterical type, Goldstein thought.

"And I pledge to maintain the secret of Oneida until it is proclaimed across the land by the liberated," the chorus repeated.

Goldstein's legs and back cramped from his position. Use the meditation practice, he reminded himself, and he concentrated on the pain until the muscles became warm and the sensations dissolved.

The rhetoric continued for two more exchanges, and then a new voice spoke. "The plan," he said, "can only succeed if we each do our part, without questions. When it is time to move, we will give the signal, from this island. In all the major cities, at the same time, we will save America. The new revolution. You are the heroes. We will set the people free."

Mad, Goldstein thought, they're all mad. He inched a few feet to the very edge of the bushes. A thorn scratched his arm and a small trickle of blood oozed toward his hand. He held his fingers to the cut and applied pressure. Someone else was talking now, the voice softer than MacPherson's. The tape recorder wouldn't pick up normal voice levels from this distance. He had to get closer.

He wriggled on his belly, dry twigs crackling under him as he went. The grass formed a trail behind him, crushed by his slithering weight. But the voice was becoming audible, the words more distinct as he got closer.

"And the lives that will be lost will be a small price to pay for—"

Goldstein felt prickles along the back of his neck, even before he was conscious of the footsteps behind him. He turned his head, hand on his shirt where the gun bulged just above his waist, in time to see MacPherson's towering figure looming over him, his fist wrapped around something small and round, arm raised.

"Nice to see you again, Mr. Schopenhauer," he said.

Goldstein felt a smashing pain on the side of his head, was glad that he didn't have far to fall, and then sank back into the dry grass.

# 23

"And then, when I was about ten, we moved to North Carolina. That was in the fifties, before Rosa Parks, before Little Rock. Wait a minute," he said, leaning against the handrail and holding his chest. "Couldn't they have picked a flat place to have their little insurrection?"

Carrie laughed. They made quite a rescue team, she thought—a painter from the East Coast, who thought Central Park was a fine example of rugged terrain, and an out-of-shape forty-year-old political radical. If they kept walking around the island, small as it was, they would certainly wear themselves out, and it might all be for nothing. No, they had to keep going, had to find Goldstein.

"We should have taken something to drink," she said. She rested against a fern-covered embankment and looked out over the brilliant bay to the hills marching upward, like a Chinese landscape.

"Okay, let's go," Mother said. "So, that's where I first woke up to how it was for a lot of people." They climbed to the roadway and stopped again.

"This is it," Carrie said, pointing to the left.

"Why?" Mother asked, looking the other way. The road sloped slightly downhill to the right, but began a gentle climb in the direction Carrie had suggested.

"Don't know. Feels right," Carrie said, starting off toward the curve. "Trust me."

"I'd trust you better downhill," he said, laughing as he caught up to her. "Don't go so fast."

"We're already an hour behind them. I wish we had been able to get in touch with Cruz. Finding them isn't going to be easy," she said, frowning.

"There will be a sign." Mother rolled his eyes heavenward. "Do you mind if I stop now?" he asked, hitting a stride of long, even steps.

"What do you mean?" Carrie said, struggling to keep up with him.

"Talking. I'll tell you my whole fascinating story later. I can move better if I'm not reciting, too."

They continued on, ignoring the trails that wound farther up the hill, and stayed on the main road by silent agreement. Carrie concentrated on maintaining her pace. The road was nearly empty. Two young couples walked by, arms entwined, chattering and laughing loudly. A white-haired woman in baggy pants strode past them, her purple hat flapping as she bounced along. Mother and Carrie walked a little faster. An open truck, loaded with branches and shrub clippings, blocked the right half of the road, and they passed it hurriedly.

"See, all that speed was only for show." Mother pointed to the woman and her purple hat, both seated quietly on a bench overlooking the water. "We may not be faster, but we'll get where we're going."

"If we only knew where that was." Carrie looked ahead to a cluster of buildings. "There," she said, running toward the bench. "Look!"

She stopped in front of the woman. "Excuse me," she murmured, reaching behind the woman's legs and pulling out a crumpled roll of black. Mother came up behind her, and she unrolled the sweatshirt. A baseball cap tumbled out and Carrie caught it before it hit the ground. Sewn inside the sweatband was a label. *JG*. In fancy script. Carrie shivered. If this was a sign, it wasn't a good one.

> Bound and gagged and slumped under a heavy beam. Blond hair sticky with spider webs, leaves clinging to his eyelashes, blue eyes filmed with pain. No movement. No sound.

"What now?" she asked, as they walked back to the path.

Mother grabbed her arm and led her to another bench. "I'm thinking that our friend may be in some discomfort." He sat still, but his eyes were in constant motion.

Come on, Carrie thought, do something. We need to do something.

"We'll just have to keep going. Sitting here buys us nothing." He fingered the baseball cap. "A's. I didn't know he was an A's fan."

Carrie was afraid—afraid for Goldstein the person, and afraid for Goldstein the detective, who might prove that Tricia didn't kill Hawkins.

"Check that out," Mother said, pointing to the largest building in the complex, about a hundred yards away. Five men were coming out of a door, walking down the steps, heading for the path. A sixth man remained on the steps, a pair of binoculars dangling from his neck.

"The one in front looks like the manager of the house across the street," Carrie said. "His name is Khamir. I've seen him before, talked to him in the grocery store. And two of the others—they live there, too."

"I'll wager I know where our friend is," Mother said, turning so that only his back could be seen from the roadway.

"So what do we do now?" Carrie asked. The five men were standing at the foot of a trail that went down toward the water.

"We could start a fire near the building, flush them out,"

Mother said, "but someone might get hurt. Maybe we could bribe that guard."

"Maybe," Carrie answered, "but we might end up keeping Goldstein involuntary company. They're going down to the beach," she said, as the group walked off. The guard picked up the binoculars and appeared to be following the men as they walked down the narrow trail.

"Listen, here's what we do," Mother said. He rolled the sweatshirt around the cap and laid the bundle on the bench. "You go back down to the picnic area, find a ranger. Tell him the truth, and get him to stop all the departing ferries until we get there. Call Cruz again, and tell him what's going on." He turned his head slightly, until he could see the building; the guard was still looking through the binoculars. "Just go back the way we came, fast as you can," he said, standing and brushing off the seat of his pants.

"And what are you going to be doing?" Carrie asked. "I get to deliver messages and what do you do?"

"My dear lady," Mother said, "if we could trade places for this little number, I would surely love to arrange it. But they know you and they don't know me, and that's what's going to save our mutual friend."

"I don't know if I'd call him my friend," Carrie called over her shoulder. She began to run, away from the building, saving her energy because she knew how far she had to go.

# 24

Goldstein's head ached from the blow, and his wrists and ankles hurt from the rope with which he was bound. A wad of cloth was stuffed into his mouth, another strip tied around his eyes. Movement was impossible, but he could identify voices. He listened hard; the conversation was sporadic and unrevealing, mostly talk about jobs and the weather. Where is the tape recorder? he wondered.

"I am proud of you all. This is proceeding very well, and it is a good omen for the liberation action." Rolled Rs. MacPherson, for sure. "There's a bit of bad business that I want to clear up once and for all. You can lay the question of Clifford Hawkins to rest. I know that some of you have some fancy ideas, but Oneida did not kill Clifford Hawkins. We would never sanction an action that would so foolishly call attention to ourselves. If we were going to remove a soldier from the ranks, we wouldn't do it in our own front yard, so to speak. Is that clear?"

Sounds of acknowledgment. What a waste of a fine Friday afternoon, Goldstein thought. Well, at the least, these maniacs will be stopped and San Francisco will still be here tomorrow. And maybe I'll still be there to see it. Assuming that Ronson gets it together.

A gravelly voice with a middle-European accent stopped

in midsentence. "Hey, see that skinny guy coming across the field?" Footsteps sounded on the concrete floor.

"Doesn't look like anyone I know." MacPherson. "Okay, take positions." There was a scramble and clatter, people moving in different directions.

"Tall," said the Spanish accent.

Goldstein lay there listening, hoping that it wasn't some innocent person who had stumbled into the area unwittingly, wishing MacPherson and his troops would show restraint.

Another voice, Italian perhaps. Soft quality. "We can't let him get up here. All the maps, the radio equipment—"

"Not to mention our extra baggage." MacPherson. "Gino, go down and find out who he is. Keep him away from here. The rest of you, hold your positions. We don't want to be picking up any more flotsam." Goldstein winced as a foot kicked him in the back.

Meditate, he told himself, and think. But he wasn't accustomed to the pain and the difficulty of breathing. It wasn't working. There was another flurry of movement; Gino's footsteps receded. The room was still, and Goldstein pictured the scene: men in guerrilla fatigues, bent at the windows with their semi-automatics. No, they'd be wearing corduroy slacks and wool sweaters, this bunch. Someone coughed and was admonished for making noise.

"He's talking to Gino." Jamaican whisper.

"Look, the black guy's pointing to something." The Spanish voice.

"I don't like this." MacPherson, alarmed.

Goldstein tensed and released his muscles, repeated the exercise several times. Sensation slowly returned to his arms and legs, and he felt the cold of the floor through his thin shirt.

"He's coming up with Gino." MacPherson, commanding. "Be prepared to shoot if I give the signal." Clicks of safeties undone, then footsteps up the metal stairs.

"Stop right there," MacPherson said. "Gino, come all the way in. You, stay where you are."

"He's from National," Gino said. "Says he has orders to take the prisoner with him. Says that Khamir radioed ahead, got a boat coming to the dock to pick them up."

There was silence. Goldstein decided that he definitely could wait to find out what was in store for him at Oneida's national headquarters. If he made it that far without being pushed over the side of the boat. Some poor old man, out for a morning walk, would find his body on a breakwater, bloated and bleached.

"Did he show you proof?"

"Hey, babe, how do you think I got here if I'm not from National?"

Goldstein's heart pounded. He almost grinned through the cloth stuffed in his mouth. Mother. Crazy, but it might work.

"I've seen him at headquarters." The Spanish voice. "He's all right." The boy who experienced paradise in the physics lab. It had to be the boy who wanted out. Good for you, Goldstein thought. I owe you one.

"I never saw him," the Scandanavian voice objected.

"Listen, babe, I don't stay in one place too long. Too much to do, too many places to go. If he saw me and you didn't, what's the difference? Now, I have to get going."

"First I'm going to send a courier to Khamir and check your story." MacPherson. Brighter than I thought, Goldstein noted ruefully. "We wait, and if the answer is good, then you both leave. Otherwise, you join him on the floor." The thinking man's revolutionary.

"Okay," Mother said, "you do that. But if I don't get to the boat with him in time for the helicopter they have waiting for us, they're going to be mightily annoyed." Another silence.

"Take him," MacPherson said. "If this is funny, if it isn't right, you'll feel the full power of Oneida."

"You should be very careful about who you threaten," Mother said. Goldstein could picture his face, fierce and scowling, the way it looked when his king was endangered. "You, untie his hands and feet. Don't want to alarm the tourists." Goldstein thought he would spring up when the bonds were finally cut, but he had to move slowly because of the stiffness. He rubbed at his wrists, then his ankles; sensation was returning.

"Good. Take the gag out." Mother was giving the orders now. Suited him well, Goldstein thought. His jaws ached from being forced open for so long. Hands from behind started to untie the blindfold. "Leave it, you fool," Mother commanded. "If he lives, you don't want him to be able to identify you all, now do you? Okay, now you, take anything that belongs to him and help me down the stairs with him." Goldstein heard someone walk away; whoever else was in the room was still, neither talking nor moving.

"And I don't want to hear anything from you," Mother said into his ear. "Do you hear me?" Goldstein, still blindfolded, wasn't sure if Mother had been talking to him. "Hey, you with the rag over your eyes. I don't want any funny moves from you or you'll end up looking like one sorry bag of potatoes. Now tell me, do you understand?"

Goldstein spoke to the air in front of him. "Tell your friends they have very bad manners."

The blow surprised him, a flat-handed slap across the face. It stung, brought tears to his eyes, but it also helped get his blood moving again.

"Just don't play any more games and we'll be fine," Mother said, propelling Goldstein in front of him with a shove. He grabbed Goldstein's shirt and yanked him to a stop. "Hey, where's the kid with his stuff?"

"I'm coming," the Spanish voice said. "Had to find his tape recorder."

Mother kept his hand on Goldstein's back as they walked down a flight of stairs. At the landing, he removed the blindfold; Goldstein couldn't see a thing for several seconds, and Mother poked him in the back, a signal to move forward again. They stepped out into the glaring sunshine, and Goldstein stumbled but managed to regain his balance. The boy standing next to Mother was his moon-faced would-be messenger on the ferry.

"No tricks, wise guy." Mother stood in front of him, looking back up the stairs. Someone must be watching them, Goldstein realized. They marched out to a narrow cement walk that connected to the blacktop road.

"I'm gonna lead," Mother said quietly. "You walk behind me, steady and not too fast, and don't look back. We don't want any pillars of salt on this trip."

Mother started off and Goldstein followed. His legs were stronger now and his eyes could again see more than shapes and shadows.

"Tell the boy to give me back my gun," Goldstein whispered.

"Pass me his stuff," Mother said to the boy. "The man don't feel right without his protection." Mother stopped short, and Goldstein bumped into him, retrieving the gun and slipping it into the waist of his pants, under his shirt. This is really going to work, he thought. Piece of cake.

"Okay, babe, we move a little faster now. We'll be at the road in a few seconds. When we pass that curve up ahead, we're gonna pour it on. I want to put distance between us and those dudes. They're nasty."

Goldstein nodded and they cleared the edge of the path and stepped onto the blacktop. A pair of joggers, two women in warm-up suits, ran by and looked at them, one turning her head to glance back after they passed. Goldstein examined his pants, covered with dust and grease. Ah well, he concluded, you can't always make a good first impression.

Still in formation, they picked up the pace a little. The boy, a pudgy fellow with a flattop haircut and dimples, looked scared. They were approaching the bend in the road, and Goldstein prepared for the next phase. His mind started racing with plans, working on what he had to do when they got back to the dock. Call the Coast Guard, call Intelligence, call Cruz, get the park rangers in on things. This isn't over yet, he thought.

They walked around the bend, and Goldstein waited for Mother's signal to move out. He felt fully recovered now, and he guessed that it was slightly more than a mile to the picnic area. Easy.

"Okay, let's open it up," Mother said, and they began to run.

"Just pretend to be having fun," Goldstein said. "Nobody pays any attention to joggers."

They formed a rank, running together down the wide road toward the stairs, toward escape. The boy was red-faced and puffing, but kept up with them. The rest was all downhill. Gutsy of Mother, but it was working.

He felt good, into his stride, the training paying off again. Considering the time he had spent tied up, circulation slowed, he had come back quickly and was taking long, easy steps toward safety. Mother was right beside, the boy two paces behind. The road stretched out straight in front of them for twenty feet, then made a sharp turn to the left. They were almost at the steps that led to the dock. He felt strong, confident, and ran with the first pleasure he had felt in hours.

He made the left turn, leaning slightly into the hill and then stopped short, blood pounding. Ten feet ahead of him in the middle of the path was Khamir, with three of his men. There was no time to think; instinct and his police training would have to do it for him. He looked around—no one else in sight, no joggers, no kids skipping school. Mother pulled up short beside him. They had a better than fair chance to take the group. He was in top condition, Mother was big, and the boy was scared. That added up to a lot of adrenaline.

"Hey," Khamir said, "where do you think you're going?"

Goldstein felt for his gun. A young woman with a baby in a papooselike contraption on her back came up the stairs and paused to catch her breath. He let his hands drop to his sides.

Mother strode up to Khamir. "I've got orders to take him to the ferry. From national headquarters," he said. There was only a short distance between them and the stairs, but Khamir was in the middle of the path. Mother had better make this one work as well as the first one. MacPherson had been too easy.

"Who gave the orders?" A placid expression came over Khamir's face as he licked the bottom of his mustache. Soong, Sanchez, and their Nigerian housemate all followed the discussion as though it were a ping-pong match.

"I told you. National headquarters. And if we miss the ferry, it won't be my fault." Mother gave Goldstein a shove. "Let's go."

Khamir, all five feet five of him, stood his ground. "No, you aren't going anywhere. The ferry isn't due for another forty minutes, so there's no hurry, my friend." He nodded at Soong, who reached into his pocket and took out a snub-nosed revolver. This was getting serious. "Please. First prove what you are saying. If I'm wrong, then I will be happy to take any blame for your lateness."

Mother scowled and looked around. Goldstein kept his eyes on the woman, who had taken her baby out of the carrier and was calmly changing his diaper on a bench. No guns. A diversion, a fight, yell for help. The boy who had accompanied them was just standing there, shaking and breathing hard. He wouldn't be much help.

"You're getting me mad, babe," Mother said. "Tell your boy to put his toy away. We've got to get going."

"Put your hands behind your backs, all three of you," Khamir said. "We're going back to the garrison, and we don't want any innocent bystander to get hurt, now do we?" He looked over at the young woman, who was stuffing a diaper into a plastic bag. "Soong will be right beside me, and the gun is in his hand, pointed right at our fair-haired friend." Goldstein clasped his hands lightly together behind him and started walking, Mother on one side of him, the boy on the other. Where are the guys in the suits now, when they could be doing something useful, he wondered.

They walked back the way they had just come, marching silently in two groups of three. The first building of the garrison loomed ahead, and Goldstein thought about his father, regretted not having made peace with him. He looked at the hills and the sea and the birds. Everything was fresh, the air was sweet, life was sweet. For how much longer, he mused, not hearing the trucks come up, one from the rear and one in front.

"Halt. This is the FBI," the voice boomed. "You in the blue sweater, throw the gun to the ground." The cavalry had come through after all, sunglasses and all. Doors slammed and Goldstein turned around. Four men and two women in park uniforms advanced toward them, guns extended. Carrie Rayborn hopped down from the cab of the truck. Soong looked to Khamir, waiting for orders. Three more rangers moved in from behind, and a police helicopter approached from the south, directed by Ronson's crackling radio.

"I repeat, throw down the gun and any other weapons." The nine rangers were getting closer, moving steadily toward them. "Oppressors of the people," Khamir screamed and grabbed the gun from Soong. When he made his move, Mother lunged and dove for Khamir's ankles and dropped him with a splat to the blacktop. Goldstein removed the gun from Khamir's struggling grasp, and Mother got up, dragging Khamir to his feet. Soong and his companion were being marched to one of the trucks. Two more trucks rolled to a stop and twelve men circled the garrison building in which MacPherson and the others were still hiding.

"You're determined to keep me in your debt, aren't you," Goldstein said to Mother, who was grinning broadly. "I'm grateful."

"The time will come when you can thank me properly," Mother said. "I'll hold your marker until then."

"Ironic, isn't it?" Goldstein said, watching as the first truck pulled away. "Homicide detective endangers lives, uncovers a nest of terrorists, but doesn't solve his case. They didn't kill Hawkins. MacPherson said so inside, when he thought I was unconscious, and it sounded like the truth. But you really did a good job."

"And this lady here didn't do too bad either," Mother said, putting an arm around Carrie. "Good thing she came with me."

Goldstein looked at Carrie. Her pants were covered with a layer of red dust, her long hair was escaping from the pins that were meant to hold it back, and her left cheek had a grease smudge that went all the way to her nose. It was the first time Goldstein had seen her smile.

"This was kinda fun," she said. "Look at the powers of persuasion I have." She swept her hand in a wide circle at the scene, a landscape now dotted with trucks, helicopters, and park employees.

"I do appreciate it," Goldstein said, brushing a piece of straw from her hair. "I am worth so much more alive than otherwise. What we need is a celebration."

Carrie hesitated. "I can't celebrate yet. My daughter's problems aren't over. If Oneida didn't kill Hawkins, then who did?"

# 25

Carlos Cruz noiselessly opened the door to his sons' bedroom and stepped inside. The shaft of light from the hall shone on the bunk bed where Carlos Jr. and Julio slept. Cruz picked up the model airplane from his son's desk and ran his hand along the bump of glue at the wing joint. If Julio was in trouble, what would Junior do? Would he tell the police where his brother was hiding? Would he help him escape to start a new life? There was no way to know. The ties run too deep and the situation wasn't covered by your average Sunday school sermon. Morality stopped following rules when you were talking about your flesh and blood. A brother. A son. A daughter. Tricia Rayborn would get probation for the car theft, and would probably go on to fulfill whatever her life ambitions were. Her mother had stuck with it; without Carrie Rayborn and the photographs, without seeing the dog at the Kerner house, he might never have believed that it was Royal.

Would Royal really have allowed Tricia to go to jail for his crime? And it *was* Royal who made that phone call—unless someone besides Royal Kerner would have called Clifford Hawkins a thief. Royal stole the Buick, had a rifle and the dog with him, shot Hawkins, and then ditched the car. Tricia Rayborn just happened to steal the wrong vehicle. And then Royal deposited rifle and dog at his grandmother's house, waited for the streets to clear, and went home. He had taken the ultimate responsibility, Cruz thought, recalling Royal's words at the soccer practice. He had saved the world from Clifford Hawkins's evil. Unless I'm wrong, Cruz thought.

Cruz leaned over and pulled the covers up to Julio's chin, touching the boy's soft hair. My sons, he thought, will be full participants. They will be educated, they will know how to get what the world has to offer them, know how to use their talents. He knelt beside Carlos Jr. and looked at the boy's face. His expression, even in sleep, was one of satisfaction, of being comfortable in his own skin.

Which Royal Kerner was not. Even at the soccer game, distracted as he was by Danny's injury, Cruz had sensed Royal's apartness. And all his quotes. Goldstein would have caught on sooner, would have picked up the significance of Royal's concern with good and evil, with responsibility, and would have seen him for what he was—a boy who had moved too fast into a world he wasn't prepared for. One foot in a life where people like Clifford Hawkins assaulted children and old ladies, the other in a realm of abstract ideas that he had no background to understand. A father who had died and left Royal to be the man of the house, to take care of his mother and grandmother.

It will be different for my boys, Cruz vowed, as he closed the bedroom door behind him. He put on his dark windbreaker, kissed Elenya good night, and locked the door of the apartment.

Cruz moved his legs again, uncrossing them, and pulled the collar of his jacket closer. The nights are always cool this time of year, he thought, as the last light went out in the Kerner house. Almost midnight. Maybe the girl was telling the truth and the San Francisco police just hadn't found

Royal yet. He took another bite of the salami sandwich he had brought with him.

Angel Island—more exciting than this, Cruz thought. Better than sitting here and waiting to do something you don't want to do, that you don't even know will happen. He had laughed with Goldstein over the captain's change of heart. He had been furious at first, but that turned to silence when the evening news portrayed Goldstein as a hero who almost single-handedly prevented possible loss of life by stopping a group of crazed terrorists. That's the breaks, he thought, and recognized a pang of jealousy.

He wrapped the remainder of the sandwich and put it back in his pocket, and saw the slim form of Jessica Kerner slip out the back door, a bulky object on her back. A pack, by the shape of it, probably stuffed with food and clothing. This is it, he thought, palms sweating and heart pounding.

The girl closed the door quietly and was headed for the fence, the same one that Royal had vaulted earlier in the day. If he kept still, she wouldn't see him, hidden as he was by a large lilac bush. She dumped the pack over the fence, then swung herself up and over as easily as her brother had done, and landed on her feet, not more than a yard away.

The girl bent down and slipped her arms through the straps of the pack. She walked purposefully through the yard and out onto the street. Cruz made sure that she was well onto the sidewalk before getting up himself. He would have to follow at a good distance so that she wouldn't be aware of him.

They walked for several blocks, Cruz taking care to keep to the shadows and maintain four house-lengths between them. His sneakers were noiseless, and the girl must have been so lost in her own thoughts that she didn't notice when he stepped on a piece of glass. The crunching sound seemed to Cruz to echo through the street, but the girl kept going. An occasional flash of headlights lit up the street and then darkness returned. Cruz realized the girl was headed for the Mills College campus.

She stopped once to adjust the pack, then resumed her steady, unhurried pace. The campus was only one block away now, and Cruz felt the clammy sweat on his forehead. Better, he thought, to be home in bed next to Elenya, listening to the rhythmic sounds of sleeping children. But he had to do this.

"Psst. Royal. Where are you?" the girl said in a loud whisper. She was standing beneath a large maple tree, the pack now resting on the ground. He must have run away before, just as she had said that morning. She knows exactly where to go, Cruz thought. She walked in a widening circle, repeating her stage whisper and waiting for an answer. Cruz hung safely back in the shadows.

"Royal, you gotta come out now. I have food and clothes and money for you. You can get pretty far away, but I gotta talk to you. Come out."

There was no answer, no sound, no movement. Cruz remained hidden behind a box hedge that bordered a path between two darkened buildings. The girl was becoming more agitated, her voice louder and more frantic.

"Royal, I know you're here. It's all right to come out. Nobody knows I'm here and I gotta make plans with you." She widened her circle and kept calling his name. No response. Either the boy wasn't there or else he had seen Cruz tailing Jessica. In the first case, there was nothing to do but follow her back home and hope that Royal would reveal himself somewhere along the way. In the second case, he could wait for the boy to take the chance and come out of hiding, for Jessica's sake.

There was another choice.

He stood up and moved toward the girl with his gun drawn, making sure that the safety catch was secure before he pointed it straight ahead.

"Okay, Jessica, put your hands in the air and stand still," Cruz said, loud and clear. The girl whirled around at the sound of his voice, and he advanced toward her. Even in the dark, he could see that her eyes were large with fright.

"We found your fingerprints on the gun that killed Clifford Hawkins. I'm arresting you for his murder. Let's go." He took out the handcuffs from his jacket pocket and stepped closer, close enough to smell her powdery perfume and feel the emanations of her fear.

"Why did you kill him, Jessica?" Cruz said as he held her thin wrist in one hand and the handcuffs in the other. The girl, shaking and trembling, didn't speak. Suddenly a branch snapped behind him. Cruz spun around, gun and handcuffs still in his hand. Royal stood ten feet away, a large board in his hand.

"Put it down, Royal," Cruz said. "I'm taking your sister in, and if you want to go with me, you can come along." The blood drummed in his ears. This is wrong, he thought. It's all wrong. These children should be home sleeping, dreaming. The boy held the board in front of him with both hands, his eyes shifting from Cruz to Jessica.

"Okay, man, one more time. Drop the board, and then walk around and stand next to your sister." Cruz waved the gun in Jessica's direction. Lord, don't let me shoot one of these children, he prayed. His concentration wavered and, for a moment, he thought about letting them run away. What's the matter with me? he thought. The boy is a killer.

"Why did you kill Hawkins, Jessica?" Cruz shouted, kicking up the tempo.

"She didn't. I did. Let her go and I'll drop the board." Royal swung at Cruz, missing by inches. Jessica remained frozen.

"No he didn't. I did it. You let him go and I'll come with you," she said.

Oh shit, thought Cruz. I don't need this.

"Don't, Jess," Royal said gently. "It won't work. Your

fingerprints aren't on the gun. You can't drive a car, Jess. That's how Hawkins was killed, remember? You run, go back home."

"No," Jessica said. "I'm staying with you." In the light of a passing car, Cruz saw the tears coursing down her cheeks.

"You get out of here. I already made it bad enough for one person. But that was her own fault. *I* stole the car because I had a mission. She was just being weak, giving in to her impulses."

"Is that why you made that phone call, Royal? Because Tricia was weak, and it was okay for her to take your rap?"

"You didn't know, did you?" Royal taunted. "I jived you good. You're not too bright—sucker." The board whistled past Cruz's head again. "Go home, Jess."

"No. You're in trouble and I'm staying with you. Why, Royal? How could you do it?" She tried to speak, but only a sad, choked sound came out.

"Don't you see, Jess? I did it because it had to be done. Hawkins was evil, and I removed him from the world, so that he couldn't hurt anyone else." The boy sobbed and threw down the board, and Cruz saw the tears streaming down his face. Jessica ran past him to Royal, and they clung together, crying, holding on to each other. Cruz took a deep breath and tried to push his own tears back, found that he couldn't stop them, and cried with them, standing alone in the dark under a tree on the college campus.

# PART

# 7

# SATURDAY

# 26

Her ankle still hurt when she stood on it. She tried to hobble without the crutches, found that it didn't work, and gave in. She stood in front of the open closet, looking over the selection. She was going to go to her graduation and walk, on crutches if need be, down the aisle with the others. She would brave the stares and whispers and take her place among them.

She would not sit beside Angela.

She would sit with Momma. Momma wasn't perfect, but why should she be? We are different, she thought, but I hope I have her courage, her loyalty, her resilience.

And Twink would be there. He kept her smiling, called her every day. Maybe they wouldn't spend the rest of their lives together, but she would always remember how he stood by her.

Goldstein wouldn't come, she knew. She wouldn't see his piercing eyes again, but the memory of his belief that she didn't kill Clifford Hawkins was enough.

Cruz wouldn't come, either. He might not have seen the signs that pointed to Royal Kerner if he hadn't kept his mind open. His face, when he came to the apartment that morning to tell her he was glad that it was over for her, was beautiful in a way she hadn't noticed before—sad, kind, deep.

Maybe, she thought, I can wear the blue dress to my graduation and the yellow one to my trial.

## About the Author

Marilyn Wallace lives in California with her husband and two teenage sons. She is the daughter of a former New York City policeman. A CASE OF LOYALTIES is her first novel.